DANCE in the Dark

CONFESSIONS: BOOK ONE

CHRIS ALAN

With

NYT and USA Today Best Selling Author

MELODY ANNE

Dance in the Dark
Confessions: Book One

ISBN-13: 978-0692921487
ISBN-10: 0692921486

Edited by Karen Lawson and Renita McKinney
Cover Image Provided by Frag Hunter www.sleepyg.co.uk

www.melodyanne.com
Email Melody: info@melodyanne.com

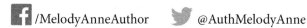 /MelodyAnneAuthor    @AuthMelodyAnne

Email Chis: authorchrisalan@gmail.com

 /AuthorChrisAlan

Printed in the USA

DEDICATION

This is an adventure I never thought I would take. Though there are many I'd love to dedicate this to, the person who gave me the belief and work ethic that made me the man I am today is my father. Thank you for always believing in me and standing by my side. I dedicate this book to you, Dennis – Love Chris

OTHER BOOKS BY Melody Anne

THRILLERS

CONFESSIONS:
*Dance in the Dark - Book One
*TBA - Next Book in the Series

ROMANCE

THE ANDERSONS:
*The Billionaire Wins the Game
*The Billionaire's Dance
*The Billionaire Falls
*The Billionaire's Marriage Proposal
*Blackmailing the Billionaire
*Run Away Heiress
*The Billionaire's Final Stand
*Unexpected Treasure
*Hidden Treasure
*Holiday Treasure
*Priceless Treasure
*The Ultimate Treasure

BABY FOR THE BILLIONAIRE:
*The Tycoon's Revenge
*The Tycoon's Vacation
*The Tycoon's Proposal
*The Tycoon's Secret
*The Lost Tycoon
*The Tycoon's Takedown - *Fall 2017*

SURRENDER:
*Surrender - Book One
*Submit - Book Two
*Seduced - Book Three
*Scorched - Book Four
*TBA - Book Five - *Fall 2017*

FORBIDDEN SERIES:
*Bound -Book One
*Broken - Book Two
*Betrayed - Book Three
*Burned - Book Four

UNEXPECTED HEROES:
*Safe in His Arms - Novella - Baby, It's Cold Outside Anthology
*Her Unexpected Hero - Book One
*Who I am With You - Novella - Book Two
*Her Hometown Hero - Book Three
*Following Her - Novella - Book Four
*Her Forever Hero - Book Five

BECOMING ELENA:
*Stolen Innocence
*Forever Lost
*New Desires

TAKEN BY A TRILLIONAIRE:
*Xander (Ruth Cardello)
*Bryan (J.S. Scott)
*Chris (Melody Anne)
*Virgin for the Trillionaire - Ruth Cardello
*Virgin for the Prince - J.S. Scott
*Virgin to Conquer - Melody Anne

FINDING FOREVER SERIES:
*Finding Forever
*Finding Each Other - *Winter 2017*

THE BILLIONAIRE AVIATORS:
*Turbulent Intentions - Book One (Cooper)
*Turbulent Desires - Book Two (Maverick)
*Turbulent Waters - Book Three (Nick)
*Turbulent Intrigue - Book Four (Ace)

7 BRIDES FOR 7 BROTHERS:
*Luke - Barbara Freethy
*Gabe - Ruth Cardello
*Hunter - Melody Anne
*Knox - Christie Ridgway
*Max - Lynn Raye Harris
*James - Roxanne St. Clair
*Finn - JoAnn Ross

UNDERCOVER BILLIONAIRE:
*Kian - Book One (Montlake) *Winter 2017*

YOUNG ADULT/FANTASY

MIDNIGHT SERIES:
*Dusk - Book One
*Darkness - Book Two
*Dawn - Book Three
*Daybreak - Book Four

PROLOGUE

"I T'S TIME TO wake up."

Slowly, her eyelids fluttered as I took an unhurried walk around the parameter of the bed. I loved how my voice bounced back at me in this small, cluttered room. This experience was so much more than a capture or kill. There was nothing out of place, nothing left to chance. This had been planned for too long.

I stopped at the back of the headboard as I looked over it to the perfect display of her body. It was a masterpiece. The frame had been pulled into the center of the room so I could observe her from every angle. The position of the bed was slightly out of place, but other than that, it was an exact replica of the scene I needed. With the bed this way I could walk around it, circle my prey, enjoy every moment of this night. There could be no mistakes—not with this.

Her whimper, as consciousness seeped in and she realized she couldn't move her arms that were bound to the steel poles at the head of her bed, was music to my ears. She was still too drugged to understand what was happening, but I was certainly a patient man. She'd come fully awake very soon—I had the means to ensure that.

"Are you rested?"

As I said this, I moved beside her, coming into her view. From the slight stiffening of her muscles I could see she recognized my voice, but it wasn't until our gazes locked that the full impact of this moment rushed through me. However, she was still too groggy for me to play with her.

She most definitely wasn't alert enough for my liking. Within seconds of her struggle to pull her arms free, she stilled, her soulless blue gaze looking back at me in too calm a manner. Her mouth opened and her dry tongue swept across her cracked bottom lip. But even that much movement seemed to put a strain on her, and she leaned her head back and closed her eyes once more. That wouldn't do at all.

"I've got a treat for you," I assured her—and myself.

Pulling a prepared needle from the bag sitting on the end of her bed, I took off the protective cap and held it up to the light, the amber liquid reflecting from the dim lamplight casting shadows in the room. She didn't bother reacting to my words so I decided not to talk for now as I brought the sharp point to her arm. She didn't budge as

I shoved the tip into her thin skin and pushed. Pulling it out, I tossed the syringe into my bag.

Taking in a heavy breath, I savored the taste on my tongue. The room was stale with a strong odor of generic cigarettes and cheap whiskey hanging heavy in the air. Though that might be unappealing to most, it smelled like victory to me. I sat on the bed beside her and peeled off my gloves. I wanted nothing between her skin and mine for this perfect moment. I needed to feel everything she felt—her terror, her realization, her pain, and finally, her acceptance.

Her eyes came open again as alertness began to enter their cold depths. I didn't feel much as I watched reality sink in for her. This had to be the most aware she'd been in at least ten years. And I was the one beside her when it was happening. As she gazed into my eyes, I could not only see fear creeping into her expression . . . I could *feel* it.

I've never been a man to feel emotion; that's such a weak human thing ordinary people spout whenever they want to explain an action. What was anger? Hate? Love? Fear? I didn't understand any of it. That's why I needed to feel it through her actions, through her expressions. The more she conveyed, the more I could soak it in—and try to mirror what I witnessed in her. She didn't realize what was to come, but somewhere deep inside she had to be aware, because this wasn't the first time she'd been in this situation. Only the last time the roles had been reversed.

Though no more than a full minute had passed since I gave her the shot, it was working beautifully. I ran my finger from her bound wrist to her elbow before pulling my hand away.

"You didn't answer me," I said, my voice pleasant. "Are you rested? You will need your rest." If someone were to hear my words, they might think I was showing concern for her. Maybe in a small way I was. She *was* special to me, after all. I wouldn't be here in this moment with her if she weren't.

"Wh . . . why?" she croaked, though it was incredibly difficult to understand her words.

"You know the answer to that," I told her as I leaned over and pulled a roll of duct tape from my bag. I tore off a four-inch piece, and her eyes filled with tears. Ah, that shine was quite lovely.

"You don't have to do this," she cried, her voice raspy and weak. I bet she couldn't recall the last time she'd had anything other than drugs and booze in her mouth. That would certainly take away any energy she had to fight. It was almost no fun.

"You're correct. I don't *have* to do this," I told her as I held the black tape between my fingers. I was ready to get started, therefore I would have to muffle her cries. I was reluctant to cover her pretty little mouth since we were finally having a conversation.

Of course, we would have a revealing discussion before this night was over. I wouldn't allow it to go any other way. As I leaned over her and looked deep into her soulless eyes, I placed the tape across her lips and watched her tears instantly wet it.

"Thank you," I told her, sincerity ringing in my voice. "I can't feel without doing it through you." I leaned down and brushed her tears away before kissing the tape that was covering her mouth.

My breath warming her skin, I made a trail across her cheek and pressed my lips to her ear. I wanted the vibration of my words to travel through her. She needed to feel this moment as powerfully as I did.

"Don't you wish you'd been more careful?" I asked. I leaned back to look into her eyes as confusion lit her expression. I took my time before continuing. There was no need for me to rush. She tried again to speak to me but the tape wasn't going anywhere.

"There really isn't anywhere a person can hide their secrets. There's always somebody watching," I told her. Awareness began showing in her eyes. "I was watching that night and I remember it all . . . right down to the smallest detail. My future was shaped in those hours. Your future was, too, though neither of us knew it at the time." The horror of the past widened her eyes as she understood how she was going to pay for what she had done.

There still wasn't anger in my voice. Why should I be upset? It had been ten years since that fateful night—ten years to the day actually.

"Where should we begin?" I asked, not even trying to hide my smile. "Do you remember?"

She shook her head as her eyes pleaded for mercy. It was interesting to see this woman come back to the land of the living. It didn't change what was to come, but it was worth watching nonetheless.

The next item I pulled from my bag widened the terror in her eyes to the point she looked like a cartoon character. My smile faded as I contemplated her panic and shock.

"Why do you seem surprised?" I asked. I ran the edge of the blade between my thumb and forefinger as I caressed the eight-inch weapon. "I guess one human emotion is hope," I said, having to accept that as answer enough for her behavior. "Maybe a person truly does think they can escape the impossible. I might have to ask you if you still feel hope when you're too weak to scream any more."

I released the blade and rested it on her neck, the sharp point barely touching her pale skin. I lightly dragged the knife across her rapidly beating pulse before moving it up her cheekbone and beneath the dark skin below her eyes.

"Don't shake too hard or you might get some nicks that aren't intended," I warned.

Her body stiffened as she desperately tried not to move. I ran the blade over the curve of her nose, noting the obvious bump where it had been broken more than once. I could put the first mark there . . . but no, that's not where this would begin.

Next I rested the blade at the top of her chest, circling the sharp tip over her thundering heart. I was tempted to push it down, just enough to feel her blood rise to the surface and coat the blade in a nice shade of crimson. Instead, I moved across her chest and ran the back of the blade up her arm, over the inside curve of her elbow, and then brushed it over her wrist.

"It's fascinating how your pulse pushes outward, almost as if your body is asking me to give you a little slice to relieve the pressure, to bleed you out," I told her. "You've poisoned your blood for so long, it would probably be a relief to your body."

She whimpered and I decided the risk of getting caught might be worth hearing her pleas for mercy so I could absorb the sweet sound of her anguished screams. I left the blade resting against her wrist as I reached out and ripped the tape from her mouth.

"Please, please . . ." she immediately whimpered, the words garbled in between her sobs. "You don't have to do this. I won't tell on you. I won't."

I gazed into her eyes and tried to figure out what I was thinking about, what I was feeling. I honestly didn't know. My eyes never left hers as I moved the blade a few inches higher to where her open palm strained against the ropes securely holding her. She was tugging so hard that the rope sitting just below her wrist at the bottom of the palm of her hand was beginning to rub the skin raw.

"I don't *have* to do anything anymore," I told her. "That's one of my greatest pleasures in life. But trust me, this is a joy."

"Don't . . ." She couldn't complete the words as more sobs were wrenched from her.

It was the perfect moment to make my first cut. I didn't even have to pull the blade back before I gave it a hard thrust and felt satisfaction as it sliced through the palm of her hand.

The garbled scream escaping her throat as I twisted the blade a little to the left and then the right was well worth the tape coming off her mouth.

"You might want to pace yourself. This night is just beginning," I told her before tugging the knife free and watching the deep red blood stream down her white arm.

Yes, this night was only just beginning. I had a lot of work to complete. This is where my story begins. Maybe there's history that's led up to this moment, but this night the circle is complete. Do you want to know my story? It's not pretty. But I'm more than willing to share it with you.

CHAPTER ONE

AN ENRAGED SCREAM echoed off the small room's sterile white walls as I jolted up in an unfamiliar bed. It took a moment to realize the noise was coming from my own throat. Once the sound registered, I closed my mouth and the noise instantly halted.

The echo of feet hitting the cold, sterile floors was overwhelming. They halted and several wide-eyed medical personnel gazed at me as they checked the beeping of monitors to be sure I wasn't about to die.

What did they have to be so concerned about? Hmm, as soon as that thought popped into my head I wasn't able to hold back a smile. If I was in the room with them, they had a lot to be concerned about. My presence might not seem significant in their lives, but that could change in a matter of seconds. However, it was fortunate for them that they weren't aware of who I truly was or what it meant for me to be looking upon them. They had no idea what could come of such a meeting.

A petite redhead stepped forward, her eyes wide as she put a reassuring smile on her lips—a smile I was sure she'd given many people in positions similar to the one I was in.

"Sir, you're in the hospital."

I wanted to snap out a quick "duh" but somehow managed to stop myself. I was in a scratchy bed with blood coating my body and monitors alerting a bunch of strangers to my medical condition. It was pretty obvious where I was.

What I couldn't figure out was how I'd gotten there. I took a brief moment to close my eyes and try to think back to the last thing I could recall. I didn't like having so many eyes on me without being exactly aware of where they were and what expressions they wore. But this was important too.

It seemed rage was an emotion I was more capable of feeling lately. I thought my reactions were more controlled than this, that I wasn't such a weak human, but as I remembered what had most likely landed me in this place, fury was certainly running through my blood. That bitch—that fucking bitch.

As soon as I had that thought, I snapped my eyes open. There was no way I was allowing her to affect me in any way, especially with something as powerful as anger. Instead of focusing on her, I'd concentrate on the other people in the room. There was a story here that needed to be told—I had no doubt about it. There always was.

My advantage at the moment was the blank spots in my memory. What had happened in the last few hours? As much as I despised weakness, right now I had to act afraid, disoriented—a victim. That word made me want to puke. It disgusted me how weak so many people were. How could I respect anyone who though it acceptable to be a victim?

I couldn't. It was impossible. But it was imperative to act like a wounded soul, even if it might rip out a piece of my very essence. If I took two seconds to remember it was all part of the façade, maybe I could stomach it a bit better.

"What happened?" I asked, almost convincing myself the weakness in my voice was real. The slight scratchiness was a beautiful touch, if I did say so myself.

"What do you remember?" the redhead asked.

Looking around, I tried to gauge what they knew and what they were fishing for. There weren't any officers in the room. That was a good sign. Again a flash of anger washed through me and I had to push it down. That bitch had paid, but she'd gotten her shot in. That wouldn't happen again, that was for damn sure.

"I'm not sure." The panic rising in my voice deserved an Oscar.

"Do you know your name?" she asked. I noticed my wallet sitting in a tray on a counter across the room. I was too smart to have my real name in there so I'd give them the identity I'd assumed.

"Adam," I said, and she seemed pleased.

"Can you tell us the last thing you remember?" she asked next. I wanted to drill her, ask her how it was she decided she was the one in charge. She looked as if she was barely old enough to be standing near me in her scrubs, let alone question someone like me.

"I was out walking my dog," I said, making sure my eyes rounded as if just realizing something. "Where's Sawyer? Is he okay?" My voice rose with each word in a perfectly synced performance.

"I'm sure he's okay," the redhead said with sympathy. "Right now let's focus on you."

"I don't care about me," I told her, forcing my heart rate to escalate. The monitors gave a warning that made the redhead's forehead wrinkle with concern.

"We can more effectively help you if we understand what happened," she tried again.

"I don't know!" I yelled. She took a step closer instead of retreating, which I found interesting.

"What we do know is there's been an accident," she softly said, her blue eyes wide, full of sympathy I didn't want nor give a shit about. I fought down a smile as I imagined reaching over and grabbing that delightfully available ponytail she was sporting and smashing her face down against my knee.

I was already covered in blood—not only mine. I wouldn't mind adding this sweet little bitch's red plasma to the mix. But this wasn't the time, and *certainly* not the place.

"Accident?" I asked instead.

I looked away from the redhead, though I found it slightly difficult to do. She was a sweet little piece of candy who I most certainly wanted a taste of. At that thought

I licked my dry lips. The taste of pennies had disappeared. Someone had obviously cleaned my face. I scanned my memory again to try to fill in the holes. If I could have a few minutes alone I was sure it would come back to me, dammit!

The next few minutes went back and forth with several of the personnel trying to dig information from me, and me acting more and more confused and frustrated. I was growing bored with this game. At last the redhead sighed, and I knew she was giving up. Finally!

"We've called someone in who will be better at speaking with you about this," the redhead told me. She seemed upset at her inability to help me. She should be ashamed. What kind of nurse was she? Maybe they'd chosen the wrong person to take the lead. I so wanted to say these things to her, but managed to keep the words inside for the sake of appearances.

The room was awkwardly silent as we waited for this new person to arrive. The young nurse shifted on her feet and I had to look away from her before the lust showed in my expression. She would make such an easy target, and her blood would blend so perfectly into that silky red hair. Tempting, it was so damn tempting.

Before my thoughts were able to stray too far down that road, the door to my room opened, sending an insignificant breeze inside. The nurse's hair feathered the tiniest bit, but that was all it took for *her* scent to drift over me.

I inhaled deeply and captured her eyes. I couldn't help the slight lifting of the right corner of my mouth. I held her surprised gaze prisoner, and I knew I owned her. Yes, she was mine right then and there—and we both knew it.

Her breasts rose as she took a deep breath. Unable to let it out, her pulse quickened, pushing against the delicate white skin of her neck, and her tongue swept across her chewed bottom lip. If it were only the two of us in the room, her fate might have been sealed before I managed to stop myself. But before I did something foolish, a new scent drifted over me.

Suddenly I lost all interest in my sweet little ginger. I ripped my gaze from hers and looked over her shoulder, ignoring the shudder passing through her tight, lithe body, and the disappointed sigh escaping her cracked lips. I was now focused on someone else.

A petite brunette walked up to me with confident professionalism, and only the slightest hint of compassion. At least that was what she seemed to portray. In reality she was probably scared. She covered it well, but I could practically *taste* fear on a person. It was the sweetest of pheromones drifting from human pores.

The woman moved closer and the air shifted again, telling me a few people had left my room. It was unnecessary for so many to be in the room now since this young woman entered the domain. I *needed* to know her. She stopped at the side of my bed, and I couldn't look away from her eyes, which were a vibrant blue with specks of purple in them. Very unusual . . . and incredibly intriguing.

Her scent was a subtle lilac that was oddly appealing. The tiniest trace of sweat beaded at the top of her forehead but was barely noticeable to anyone else. I instantly wanted to run my tongue from the edge of her jaw all the way to her hairline to get a taste of her. Too bad that would have to wait.

"May I touch your hand?" she asked, her voice melodic, soft, and warm. It was a tone she'd spent many hours practicing—professional, yet caring, soft, and understanding. She didn't know anything about me. She *couldn't* care about my needs, but the way she held my gaze and waited for permission to touch me showed everyone she thought she could pull off her little act. I looked at her hand and noticed she didn't wear a wedding ring. That was good.

"No," I said. She hadn't earned the right to touch me yet. I always insisted on providing the first caress. It was how I marked them. She wasn't mine yet, but the possibilities were definitely stirring in my mind—and my body.

"I understand," she said, not seeming at all offended. Why should she be? I was nothing to her . . . yet. That would soon change.

"Spit it out," I told her, not holding back the intensity of my gaze.

She blinked, the only sign I knocked her off-kilter. Good. There were chinks in her armor.

"My name is Janice. I'm a psychologist," she began. I didn't so much as blink as she gazed at me. She paused and waited. She grew more nervous at the intensity of my stare. I couldn't seem to control myself, which made my brow furl. I didn't like feeling out of sorts. This bitch would pay for making me feel the puny emotion.

I wasn't going to break the silence to ask her to speak. She shifted. I wasn't sure I still wanted to play with her. Maybe she *was* too weak for me. But just as I had that thought, her shoulders stiffened, and she regained a sparkle in her eyes that excited me.

"I'm sorry, Adam, I have to share some very unfortunate news with you . . ."

Yes, Janice, let's share, shall we?

CHAPTER TWO

THE DRUGS THE hospital kept pumping into me were messing with my head. I laid in that bed in a semi-conscious state as I was taken back to a time in my life before I'd become so strong.

It was an unusually hot summer day in mid-July. Even now I can close my eyes and picture the day, the moment, *almost* the very minute like it was only yesterday. It's odd how the mind works, how we hold on to certain memories so closely, while other recollections drift away in a cool winter breeze.

I was six years old, lounging comfortably on the worn sofa when I heard my mother approaching from down the hall. Without hesitation she leaned over the back of the couch and asked me why I wasn't playing outside with the rest of the neighborhood kids. I told her it was too hot and Jimmy's mom had hollered at us to get inside before we burned alive.

It's odd, but I could picture her as young and vibrant as her bright blue eyes twinkled, and her lips turned up in a smile that always made me grin back at her.

"I could use some company while I cook," she said while squeezing my shoulders. There was nothing like the smell of fresh cookies. I didn't hesitate to follow her into the kitchen and jump onto the stool she already had waiting for me.

For the next ten minutes, she let me crack eggs and stir in sugar. Later in life I figured out she could have completed the task in a quarter of the time without my so-called help, but during this time of my life she still cared enough to make the waste of time worth it.

Mom was putting in the first batch of cookies when we heard the front door swing open. Without hesitation I jumped from the stool and ran toward the front of the house. Dad was home and it was still daylight. That never happened.

I launched myself into his arms and he swept me into the air. My dad was my hero; there was no doubt about it. When I pulled back I noticed the unusual smile on his lips. That made me even more excited.

"How's your day going, slugger?" he asked.

"It's been okay, a little boring, and because it's so hot outside no one can play for long," I replied. I didn't want to complain, but it *was* summer and being locked in the house for too long was the ultimate torture.

"Then I think you'll be happy about this," he told me as he reached into his back pocket and pulled something out.

"What is it?" I asked, stretching for it. He pulled it back and smiled. This was a rare moment indeed. Dad might have been my hero, but he didn't grin too often. His giddiness was sending my joy into overdrive.

"I got us tickets to the fair," he said as he finally handed them over.

I jumped up and down in front of him while clutching the treasure in my fingers. It felt like Christmas morning. I saw Mom enter the room with a questioning look on her face.

"What is all of this noise about?" she asked from the doorway. My dad glanced up and winked at her before turning his attention back to me. I could barely stand still I was so excited.

Dad moved over to Mom, grabbed her around the waist, and pulled her in for a kiss that made me make a face at both of them. So gross. When it appeared as if they'd forgotten me, I moved over to them and made a low growling noise in my throat. Dad turned in my direction and laughed.

"Go change your clothes. We leave in ten minutes," he told me as Mom laughed.

Mom grabbed my hand and left me at my bedroom door before slipping inside her own room. I beat her back out to the living room, but just barely. She might have been as excited as me for a family day out. Now that I'm wiser, I know why that was. Back then, I had no clue.

My pockets hung heavy from all the change I'd gathered from the small Mason jar I kept proudly displayed on my bedside table. I planned on eating as much fair food as possible, playing every single game at least once, and riding each ride that didn't try to stop me because of some stupid height rule. This night would be epic.

I didn't stop talking the entire drive to the fair, but as soon as we turned a corner and I saw the flashing neon lights surrounding the giant Ferris Wheel my words fell away. In the daytime it was beautiful. But at night it was downright magical. It was the center of the fair, the epitome of all that was right in the world—a perfect circle of happiness.

"Dad, can we go on that?" I asked as he parked the car. He pulled me from my seat and hoisted me onto his shoulders as he looked at the imposing ride.

"Do you think you're big enough?" he asked with his serious voice.

"Yes," I assured him with an emphatic nod of my head.

He looked at my mother who seemed to be considering if she thought it was safe or not. I wanted to scream out my frustration. Then she looked way up where I sat on Dad's shoulders and winked.

"I know you're big enough," she told me. My heart pounded in anticipation and utter joy.

"I guess today is all about you," my dad said before he chuckled. "We will do whatever you want."

If a person could burst from happiness I would have been a puddle on the dirty ground right at my dad's feet. That was a long time ago—a time when I could still feel emotion. I could almost feel it now when I put myself back in that place. I wanted to stop this memory but the hospital drugs wouldn't allow me to pull from it.

Hours passed as the day wore on, but it felt like mere minutes as my parents followed me from booth to booth getting food, spinning on rides, and playing game after game. I won lots of stuffed animals, but I was far too big and cool to keep such frilly things, so I gave them to younger kids who eagerly stood by with wide eyes.

Yeah, I was a hero that day.

The time came when the sun set in the sky and the Ferris Wheel's lights seemed to beam all the way to the moon as it slowly turned in the dark, cloudless sky. I approached the ride with my parents, slightly afraid, though there was no way I was admitting to that, not even under the threat of torture. I was too old to have even a little bit of fear of such a mellow ride.

Never will I forget that first time around on the big wheel. I sat directly across from both of my parents, feeling even cooler that they were allowing me my own seat. When I tore my eyes away from the view near the bottom of the ride, I turned and looked at my parents. Both of them smiled, and I knew they were enjoying our night as much as I was.

Nothing had ever been more perfect. I wanted to go again and again, but I wanted to try other rides as well. I was torn so my mom made the decision and took me to other places, assuring me we'd finish the night with the Ferris Wheel.

The night was disappearing before I was ready, and as we waited in another line, I struggled to keep my parents from knowing I had to use the bathroom. That might prevent me from at least one ride. My father laughed as he rubbed my head.

"Having problems?" he asked.

"No, I'm good," I told him.

"Come on. Let's hit the john," he insisted.

"But we've been in line forever," I whined. Yeah, I knew I was being a baby, but I didn't want to miss out on the zipper. It spun and people threw up on it. I'd been too small the year before to experience such a thrill.

"I'll hold our place," Mom said, and my dad chuckled again as he dragged me away.

"I'll wait out here," he said and I rushed inside. Of course there was a long line as there was with everything. But I did my business as quickly as possible and then rushed from the bathroom.

When I couldn't immediately find my dad I nearly panicked. Then the sound of high-pitched female laughter caused me to turn my head. I had to look twice before I realized my dad was hugging a young woman, and she had her head thrown back, her lips turned up in a beaming smile.

I must have been more tired than I realized because it looked like his hand drifted down her backside. That couldn't be right. That's what he did with my mom. I called out to him and he turned, his smile fading for a moment before he leaned into the girl who lost her smile.

It looked as if the two of them were arguing, but then she turned and left after shooting me a mean look. My dad then jogged over to me, his smile back in place.

"We'd better hurry, slugger. We don't want Mom to go on the ride without us," he said. I was confused as I stared at him.

"Who was that?" I asked while letting him drag me back to the ride.

"She was nobody, just an old co-worker, but we better not tell your mother about her because they aren't friends."

It seemed a bit odd to me, but I wasn't going to argue. As a matter of fact, I forgot all about it as soon as the zipper came into view. Mom was almost to the front of the line, and I nearly did puke before the ride was finished. It was even better than I had imagined.

We stayed that night until the crowd thinned and the fair shut down. My eyes burned and my feet ached, but I never said a word. I might not get to come back for a very long time. And this night was too perfect to end so soon. Unfortunately, like any good fairytale, all good things must stop.

I fell asleep within fifteen seconds of my dad setting me in the backseat of his truck. I barely woke as he lifted me from the car and carried me inside. Both my mom and dad took me to my room and my mom tucked a black teddy bear into the crook of my arm.

"I saved one for you," she said before kissing me on the cheek.

"I thought I gave them all away," I mumbled sleepily.

"I won this stuffy while you were getting a corn dog," she told me. "So it's special."

I grumbled something at her, but I didn't release the dang bear. My dad chuckled as the two of them walked from my room, closing the door behind them. I fell back asleep instantly, the excitement of the day completely exhausting me.

That night, instead of happy thoughts, my dreams were filled with terrible images as people shouted at one another through the fog of sleep. The woman my dad had been holding in his arms flashed before my eyes, making me stir restlessly in sleep as I tried to get away from her. My dad laughed hysterically, a sound I'd never heard before. It was a terrible dream.

I didn't know it then, but I might have changed a few things during that day had I known that night had really been the beginning of the ultimate end—an end so painful I had no other choice but to change into a new person. Now I'm grateful for that day. Back then I wasn't sure I was going to survive any of it.

CHAPTER THREE

"WE NEED TO speak to you, Mr. Smith." The officer raised his brows, looking at me as if knowing my last name was bullshit. Of course it was. They weren't allowed to know who I was. There actually wasn't a single person on this planet who knew my true identity. I would always keep it that way.

"How can I help you?" I asked. I resented them being in my presence, resented the fact they thought they had the right to question *me*. Didn't they understand who had the power in this room?

"You could tell us your real name," Officer Jackson said, no humor in his tone.

"Adam Smith," I said. I kept my voice slightly confused just to sell my amnesia story. I absolutely *hated* having to act dumb in front of these morons in blue. It wasn't as if they were worthy of my time *or* attention. But since I was locked down in this damn bed, I had no choice but to play along with their little song and dance.

"How were you injured?" Officer Jackson asked. The other man stood slightly behind him, not saying a word, not smiling, and appearing to have just as much lack of humor as his partner.

"It all happened so quickly, I'm not sure . . ." I told them, then added a cough to sell myself as weak so I wouldn't have to lie there all night while they drilled me.

Of course I remembered what happened to me that night. At least I remembered all of it until I was hit by a car and left for dead. It was almost ironic, if a person were to really think about it.

There were so many lives changed because of my existence, and then in a matter of seconds my future, along with the future of possibly hundreds of frail humans, was nearly changed because of a drunk driver or a teenage kid who was now shitting himself as he curled up in a ball in his pathetic twin bed in his mommy's basement.

The door opened and the night became a whole lot more interesting as Janice walked in, her arms crossed over her chest, a scowl on her pretty lips. The same perfume she'd worn before surrounded me, and the officers, and I noticed Officer Jackson stiffened the slightest bit.

"What are you doing in here?" Janice asked, her voice prim. The two officers stepped back so they could keep me in their line of sight while also looking at her. Jackson's partner didn't appear to like this new scenario. I was enjoying myself a lot more.

"Ma'am, this is police business," Officer Spangler said, speaking for the first time.

"I'm this man's therapist and you need to have me in the room if you're going to question him," Janice told them. She wasn't backing down. I was impressed. Her strength was such a turn on I had to shift in the bed. Maybe we could get the officers out of the room and she could help me out.

"Fine," Officer Jackson said, seeming to be the one more willing to keep the peace. "But we need you to be quiet and allow us to do our job."

Janice stared both men down before moving up beside my bed and standing so close I could reach out and grab her if I wanted to. The thought was tempting.

Officer Jackson turned back to me. "How did you get injured?" He appeared furious, some of his professional façade dropping.

I wanted Janice to myself and these men gone. So I gave them the story. "I got mugged," I told them. "It's all a little blurry, but I remember these two men coming out of nowhere and they had a knife . . ." I trailed off as I forced myself to cough again and then hold my side.

"Where did this happen?" Officer Jackson asked. He didn't appear to have any sympathy at all. But he wouldn't be left with much of a choice if he had no evidence against me.

"I don't know. I just recall stumbling down the street and then a car came out of nowhere. The next thing I remember was waking up right here."

They continued to push for several minutes until Janice stopped them. She might have been a tiny thing but she had real power in her voice when she wasn't happy.

"It's time for you to leave. He's answered everything he's capable of," she told the men, her plump chest puffing out.

"Ma'am we want to catch the men responsible for this," Officer Jackson said.

"And if he remembers anything else, I'm sure he will call you," Janice insisted.

Jackson looked at Spangler, who nodded before reaching in his pocket and pulling out a card.

"If you can think of anything else, please call," Spangler said.

"I want them caught. I certainly will," I assured the men. I wanted to give them a few hand gestures but managed to keep my annoyance contained.

They stood there several more moments, but I never broke. They had no idea where I'd received my stab wound, or who had done it, but they were left with no choice but to believe my story. With my injuries, it wasn't as if I was a threat to anyone. It was absolutely perfect.

They wanted me to continue to see the psychiatrist, though. And while they had no authority over me, the doctor had made the same recommendation, but I'd rather it was *my* choice and not court-mandated. Besides, I wanted to know this particular therapist. I *needed* to know her. We definitely shared a connection that was worth exploring. I had a lot to tell Janice. She'd certainly never met another like me.

The officers left the room and it was just the two of us. As if she was aware of the danger she was in, she moved away from me—out of my reach. I wanted to tell her no distance was far enough now that she'd come into my crosshairs.

"Are you okay, Adam?" she asked.

I lay there as she waited for me to speak. Of course I was fine, but it was better for her to think I wasn't. That would certainly garner me more sympathy—that would make it easier for me to get what I wanted from her.

The great thing about a good shrink was that they were patient, and when their client was silent they assumed it was because that person was either lost in thought or thinking of something painful or critical they needed to share. In my case it was neither. I just wasn't sure what I wanted to tell her.

Should I share any of my story with her? Should I give her enough to appease her, to make her feel sympathy? I gazed at her, wondering how much to give and how much to take. I knew how things worked in this world, and nothing was given without getting something in return.

I turned from her as if in deep thought. In reality I was thinking about that night. I was thinking about how it had all gone wrong. I wasn't going to share that with her. Janice hadn't earned *that* story yet.

The events leading up to the hit and run that had sent me into the emergency room to wake up in a hell of a bad mood were constantly sitting at the front of my mind. The night had gone just how I'd wanted until things had taken a turn I hadn't anticipated.

I had tortured *her* for hours, every slice of her flesh a precision mark, every scream from her lips perfectly in tune with the melody I was composing. And then I was getting ready to end it. She was weak, and I was done. I turned my back on her, making the foolish mistake of leaving the blood-coated blade on her chest.

It was symbolic.

I'd felt the stirring behind me before my own knife had been jammed into my back. There really wasn't much pain, more shock than anything else. I pulled away from her and knew she'd nicked my lung.

Turning, I saw the slightest trace of victory in her eyes. Yes, she knew she was about to die, but at least she'd gotten a single shot of her own in. Her frail body was coated in blood, her eyes nearly shut, and her mouth hanging open, but the last look she gave me was of triumph. I surprisingly lost my composure.

I pulled the knife from my back and didn't hesitate as I pushed it forward, sinking it deep inside her chest. I didn't pull my gaze away as her triumph faded. I held her lids open as I watched the light dim and go completely out. I knew the moment she was no longer there, felt her last breath against my cheek.

She was gone.

I didn't have time to clean myself. I was losing too much blood. I stripped my clothes, barely managing to get into the sweats I'd brought with me. There was no chance of a shirt going on. I walked from the house and got into my car. I made it about five miles down the road before swerving into a pole and knocking myself out.

When I came to I knew there wasn't much time left for me as I stumbled out of my vehicle and began walking down the street. I had to get to a hospital. I'd figure out my story later.

The last thing I remembered was hearing the screech of tires before everything went black. Then I woke up in the hospital bed, unadulterated rage flowing through me.

"I need sleep," I told Janice.

Thinking of that night had placed me in a surprisingly bad mood. I didn't appreciate the mood shift. I looked at Janice again and she hesitated. She'd have to learn to obey me immediately or I might grow impatient with her. Finally she sighed.

"I understand. This has been a long night," she said.

She gave me a hint of a smile before turning and walking from the room, giving me a delicious view of her backside. I would eagerly await our next meeting, and next time I'd certainly be more prepared.

CHAPTER FOUR

I STEPPED INSIDE THE house. It had been ten days since I left it, and the smell was the first thing I noticed. If this place had been on the well-beaten path, someone surely would have reported something amiss by now. But the woman had been reclusive, had no friends, no family, no one to know she had disappeared.

Not even a mailman came to the place, and she certainly wouldn't be expecting random deliveries anytime soon. The place hadn't had a single footstep placed on the rickety stairs in the time I'd been gone. I hadn't been worried about it. It was why I'd been able to stumble away with confidence.

I'd been in this place many times before and there was a resounding echo of lost memories that might stay with me for the rest of my life—or they might dance away in a breeze. I really wasn't sure. I didn't particularly care.

Walking across the dusty entryway floor, I acknowledged that another note had been added to my newest symphony of who I became as each circle of my past was completed. The past and the present were coming together, and I was becoming whole.

Though being inside this shell of a place left me feeling an odd sense of disconnect, it was still better than lying in that hospital bed. That place was sure to cause an outburst from me that couldn't easily be explained. The constant chatter, checkups from strangers, random people walking past my door, and the terrible food of a medical facility was enough to cause insanity to a typical person. I refuse to ever be stuck in a hellhole like that again—guaranteed.

Although, it wasn't all bad. Without being there, I wouldn't have met *her*. Janice's intoxicating scent hadn't left my nose since she had first walked into my room. Being with her for our first one-on-one meeting would only amplify my senses. I relished the moment I'd see her again. I closed my eyes and felt her essence throughout my body, sending chills straight down my spine.

Yes, she was mine.

Shaking my head, I cleared thoughts of Janice from my mind. I was in *this* house now, and there was a different woman I needed to deal with. Her empty corpse waited for me at the top of the stairs. My story was multifaceted and I had the capacity to focus on many things at once.

However, I liked giving my attention to *one* person at a time. This day wasn't about Janice, it was about *her*. It was also about reflection. It was about *this* woman's home, and it was about a previous life I chose to shed a second, a minute, and an hour at a time.

I slowly made a path through the house, looking at how it was arranged, at what looked as if it fit, and what seemed out of place. My eyes were drawn to the lumpy couch in the corner before zooming out and taking in the filthy living room she'd had no desire or ability to clean. I could clearly hear the sound of a leaky pipe slowly eroding the very bones of the house.

Every echo had a story to tell, and every item spoke of this woman's triumphs and failures. Each house whispered to a person if they were willing to listen. I'd learned long ago to sit quietly and take it all in. It amazed me how few people actually did that.

Next I approached the kitchen, one calculated step at a time, hearing each board creak beneath my heavy footsteps. I took my time opening the connecting door, almost wishing for someone to be on the other side. Of course, the room was filled with nothing but emptiness—just like my soul.

I gazed around the room, scanning from one insignificant side to the other. For a moment it almost felt as if it were only a daydream and I hadn't quite woken up yet.

That thought vanished like a puff of smoke when I looked at the ceiling where a stain had formed from the blood that had seeped through the floorboards. My fingers reached to my back as I traced over the stitches where the knife had plunged into me. Slowly, I closed my eyes and relived that night. Each victim was special, but *she* was even more so.

My stroll down memory lane ended as quickly as I'd allowed it to begin. There was work to be done. I didn't need to reminisce or relive a kill. If I wanted to feel that emotion, all I had to do was repeat the action with a new opponent, someone worthy of my time.

I knew exactly who I was and how I felt. No one would ever have control of me again. No one would ever decide my destiny. I was the one holding the power. I was the one making the decisions. As I moved toward the stairs, I almost felt as if my feet weren't touching the ground.

The smell grew stronger as I made it to the second floor. I wasn't disappointed when I saw her lying exactly where I'd left her ten days earlier. Her eyes were still open, void of life. She was nothing but an empty shell. Then again, she'd been that for a long time. In reality I'd done her a favor.

She might not see it that way, but she had been pathetic and weak and her life had held zero meaning. She was much better off not having to face this world. Maybe the cruelest of punishments would have been to allow her to live.

It didn't really matter because I would never know if that was true or not. And I didn't really care. I stepped forward and began doing what had to be done. This mess had to be cleaned up. I was ready to move on.

I didn't normally take so much time with a victim, but this had been such a long time coming that I wanted it to be perfect. She needed to have the burial she deserved. I waited until the middle of the night and slipped outside with her body. I had the perfect place for her eternal resting place.

It took a while until I found the cesspit I'd picked for her. It was a beautiful ending for a trashy little bitch like her. I smiled as I watched her sink beneath the muck.

"Goodbye," I whispered. The night was quiet, but as I closed my eyes I could almost hear a response from her. I turned and walked away. I wouldn't think of her again. *She* was dead and buried.

CHAPTER FIVE

"ADAM, ARE YOU ready to talk with me?" Janice asked.

I looked at her, keeping my expression blank. I found I wanted to share my story with her, wanted to talk to her of my victory. As I gazed at her I wondered if she could handle it. There was something about her that told me she might be able to, that she wasn't a typical whimpering female.

I leaned forward and took in her scent, inhaling deeply. Damn, she smelled good. I could imagine running my tongue down the smooth side of her neck before taking a nibble on that small indent in her shoulder while I ripped away her clothes. The desire filling me was reassuring. It had been a while since I'd felt the need to fill that particular hunger.

I didn't allow Janice to look away from me as I read her body language, noted the subtle shift of her thighs as she stirred. Yes, there was a connection between us. I wasn't sure how far or deep it went. But I knew I wouldn't have to wait long to find out.

"Are you sure you want to hear my story? This is something I've held onto for a very long time. It's a memory that refuses to let go and it's been my burden to bear," I told her, shifting the slightest bit to portray discomfort. She'd never know it was an act. I could read her, but there was no way for her to read me.

Today Janice was wearing a black skirt and fitted green blouse. My eyes raked slowly over her, from the top of her shiny hair to the soles of her respectable two-inch heels, before drawing upward again, resting for only a moment on the creamy softness of the bit of thigh she was revealing.

Janice shifted in her seat again and I fought back a smile. I was well aware of when a woman wanted me, even if she didn't *want* to feel that strong desire. There was a certain change in the air, a spark in a woman's eyes, a hitch in her breath, and a stirring in her body that she couldn't stop. Yes, this woman, who had to be barely out of psych school, was completely in over her head.

If she had been too easy to break, I wouldn't have been interested, but I also didn't want to spend a year on the task. I didn't have to. I could have her beneath me by the end of this session if I truly wanted to. But what fun would that be?

"I'm here to listen and help you, Adam. I'm not here to judge," she replied softly. "Please continue your story."

I paused a moment longer as I shifted my head and looked down. I needed to play the moment just right. I needed her to feel my pain and agony. Hmm, that was enough to make me laugh. If only I were capable of real emotion.

"I didn't grow up in a traditional sort of way," I told her, then paused once more.

The slightest bit of impatience entered her expression. I wanted to tsk at her. She'd have to learn to hide her emotions better if she wanted to stay in this job—not that it would matter by the time I was done. I smiled again.

"Please go on," she said, her composure firmly back in place.

I began the story . . .

"I first experienced death at the age of twelve. Something inside of me forever shifted on that day. What I didn't realize then was things had already been changing. This just helped push it over the edge."

"How was that?" she asked when I took too long to continue.

"I was doing what most boys did at that age: riding my bike to meet some friends so we could head to the river. Of course I was a bit behind schedule, but at that age time didn't really mean anything. Not to mention my deadbeat mother never cared where I was or when I'd be home, so I pretty much was on my own every day."

"You had a harsh relationship with your mom?" Oh yes, she wanted to talk about mommy issues. How typical of her. I was almost disappointed in her predictability.

"That's not the point of *this* story," I informed her and she seemed to shrink away at my tone. Good.

"Things certainly changed a lot from the age of six to twelve, that's for sure. There's so much to say about why they changed, but I'm not quite ready to explain what happened—not yet, at least."

I had to give her a little taste to keep her intrigued.

"But right now we need to get back to me cruising along the back roads without a care in the world. I was on my way to Joe's house, and I had to pass Miller's Pond to get there. That was a spot my friends and I'd go late at night to take a dip and drink a few beers we'd stolen from our parents' fridges. As I neared the pond, I noticed something in the water. Not thinking too much about it, I kept on riding, but all of a sudden, a blood-curdling scream filled my ears."

I took a deep breath as if I was frightened, as if I was there in that moment. I almost wished I were. So much had changed for me on that day.

"I locked my brakes and skidded to a stop before dropping my bike to the ground and running to the water's edge. I stopped as I tried to figure out exactly what it was I was seeing. It couldn't possibly be real, right? No, there was no chance of that. A young girl, no more than five or six years old, was thrashing and screaming from deep in the water, obviously struggling to stay afloat. But that wasn't the most shocking thing going on." I stopped as if this was too painful for me to continue.

"What was shocking, Adam?" she asked with almost bated breath.

"She wasn't alone."

I could see the burning in her gaze as she waited for me to continue. I drew it out just to be as dramatic as possible for her.

"Who was she with, Adam?" I understood her anticipation. I paused for another moment.

"Not far away from her was a small boat, easily within range to save the girl. There was a man in it, staring at her as she tried desperately to keep her head above the water. He stared at her and I stared at him—it was my father."

Janice couldn't manage to keep her surprised gasp from escaping. I had to look away so I wouldn't smile.

"I wanted to call out to him, to ask what he was doing. But my throat closed. I couldn't seem to find my voice. I will never forget that moment. Something inside of me shifted. The need to help the girl began fading as I watched the event unfold.

"In the past couple of years I'd most certainly had dark thoughts with all that had changed in my life, but nothing compared to what I was feeling in that particular moment. When I'd spotted the girl, my first thought had been to jump in and pull her out even if I didn't know how to swim. But then I saw my father, and the expression on his face, and that kept my feet firmly planted on the ground."

I looked at Janice now and couldn't read what she was thinking. She'd had time to compose herself. Damn! I needed to unhinge her again.

"I stepped back, hidden by the shrubbery, and watched as the girl sank below the water before her head shot back out and her cries grew weaker. I looked to my father again as the child tried to swim to him but was unable to. His lips turned up into a smile before he heard a noise on the shore. He turned quickly, his gaze scanning the tree line. I could see his relief when an old German shepherd ran out and took a drink from the water before darting off again.

"My father turned his attention back to the girl as she sank below the water once more. He was slowly moving his boat closer and I wondered if he was going to save her. I was unsure how I felt about it. She was down for several moments this time, and I wasn't sure if she was coming back out. It was suddenly so quiet that I wanted to run and hide for fear of what I was feeling."

"What did you feel, Adam?" Her voice had grown very quiet.

"I realized another shift was happening inside of me. I was *enjoying* this moment. There was something buried deep down inside of me that was awakening, and I couldn't turn away as the child popped back up for a much shorter period of time, her cries now muted by the water in her throat. I didn't look at my father anymore; my attention was focused solely on her." I hung my head as if I was ashamed. Janice said nothing this time, so I continued.

"I have no idea how long it lasted. It might have been seconds, or it might have been minutes. But soon she sank down and I waited and waited. All I saw were ripples floating away from the place she'd been, from where her body had sunk for the final time.

"I stood in my hiding place for a long while, wondering what I should do next. I was upset it was over, and I didn't have more time to process what it was that had awakened within me. But I knew I had to go before my father saw me. The girl was gone, and my friends were waiting. What if they saw my father? What if we both got in trouble? I knew we'd done something wrong even if I didn't fully understand what that was."

"Did you feel you were in the wrong?" Janice asked.

"I didn't know what I felt. But before I had a chance to run, I saw my father move over to where the girl had gone down for the last time. He reached into the water with some sort of pole and was poking around. Much to my fascination and horror, I watched as he pulled the listless body of the girl to the water's surface. He looked around the lake again, then sat there with her dangling on top of the water, her face still down."

I gazed at Janice as she stared back in disgust. I wanted to slap her for that. I barely managed not to.

"I didn't move for a good five minutes as I watched my father's face. I wanted to ask him what this was about, what he was doing, but I knew better than to do that. The father I loved and respected so much wouldn't tolerate unsolicited questions. I idolized my dad. I also knew not to make him angry. Bad things had begun happening when he was upset. Suddenly my father pulled the girl into his boat and began rowing toward the shore. I knew now was definitely the time to go."

"You never called out to him?" It might have been a question but it didn't need an answer.

"I snuck out of there quietly, jumped on my bike, and rushed to my friends. I breathlessly told them about the girl, omitting my father's part in her death, and then stood there panting as I waited for their reaction. At first they didn't believe me. But soon they realized from the tone of my voice that I wasn't kidding. Some of them were hesitant to follow me back to the pond, but others wanted to go immediately. I was afraid of my father finding out I'd seen it all."

"What did you say to them?" Janice asked.

"I told them if anyone was there, not to tell them I saw anything. Joe asked me why." I hesitated again for effect.

"And what did you answer?"

"Because I didn't save her. Then Peter pointed out that I didn't know how to swim and, on the verge of tears, I said they wouldn't believe me.

"I had to cover my tracks because if my father was still there, he definitely couldn't know I'd been there, so I told my friends my dad would be disappointed in me for not trying to help her."

"Did they continue to argue?"

"My friends immediately stopped. They knew my dad had a temper and they wouldn't be willing to set off his wrath. I never thought about it then, but none of their dads inspired fear like mine did. Today that makes me smile. A man who is feared is also a man who's respected. Weakness is for the faint of heart."

"Oh, Adam, admitting to our strengths *and* weaknesses is human," Janice said. Again I wanted to hit her, but instead I finished my story.

"We went back to the pond, and much to my surprise both my father and the girl were gone. I frantically looked around for any sign of them. I couldn't have been gone for more than half an hour. How had he left so quickly without a trace of anyone having been there? I was confused.

"My friends called bullshit on my story, calling me a liar, saying I'd definitely gotten them with that one. We were all pre-teens. Of course we lied a hell of a lot. But this time I needed them to believe me. I still remember how much I wanted to share what I'd experienced that day. I didn't realize you couldn't share that kind of experience with another person. It was something personal and unexplainable.

"I desperately searched for proof that it had happened, not only for them, but for me as well. I didn't want to think it was nothing more than a daydream. Just when I was ready to give up, I noticed a small toy on the edge of the water. I hopped off my bike, ran down the bank of the lake, and, to my surprise, it was a small doll. I grabbed it with excitement, ready to prove the assholes wrong."

"Why excitement?" she asked.

"Because I'd proven it had happened and that was important. I turned to my friends with arrogance as I held the doll up like a trophy. I could see their eyes grow bigger as they realized my far-fetched story just might be true. When I knew they believed me, I also knew we could never speak about being there again. What would happen if people knew we'd done absolutely nothing? What would happen if my father knew I'd witnessed it? Would he share with me or be furious? I was too scared to find out.

"Kimberly was the first to speak after I stopped smiling, and she asked if I thought her family would be searching for her? I told her I didn't know.

"I told my friends that what had happened stayed at the pond. We could never tell anyone we'd been there; it was between us and only us. They agreed because that's what boys did. We made pacts, and we didn't break them, even if we didn't know the reasons behind what we were doing.

"Also, I didn't want my friends to know I was becoming an entirely new person. Something had shifted inside of me and I was scared. Each of us sat silently on our bikes, wondering what our next move should be. Then we heard the name Sarah shouted from behind some trees. We looked at each other and nodded, spun our bikes around, and peeled out of there."

"Did you try to help?" Janice was definitely disappointed in me now.

"No. We just went our separate ways, our plans ruined for the day. But later that night, I lay in bed with my eyes wide open. I couldn't get the image of her falling beneath the surface of the black water out of my mind. I couldn't stop hearing her voice, the sound of her begging for her life. And I couldn't forget the look on my father's face. I'm really not sure if that was the start of a new obsession for me, or if it was what had been inside of me all along. I still don't know."

When I looked at Janice this time, I knew something had changed between us. I'd allowed her to see a little bit of the monster within me. But she wasn't afraid. She wasn't sure what she was feeling, but it certainly wasn't fear. I wanted to smile, and it took a lot for me not to.

This was getting more interesting by the second . . . definitely more interesting. I would have Janice. I would have her very, very soon.

CHAPTER SIX

NOT A DAY goes by when I don't think about her. Her hair, her eyes, her smell. I wanted to know everything there was to know. From the way she moves to how she sleeps at night. What she doesn't realize is, it's not a question of how we come together, it's a question of *when* the final dance will happen.

It took a little time and patience for me to find her outside of work. You see, she's harder to find than you'd think. So I decided I'd sit by her office and wait. And watch. Eventually she'd come out of the depressingly small space she spent her weekdays.

Just as I was thinking I might have missed her, there she was. I couldn't contain my excitement as the hair on the back of my neck rose. She affected me in ways I wasn't entirely comfortable with, but the experience of feeling these new feelings made it bearable.

I watched her climb into her car, put it in reverse, and carefully back out of her spot. Once she was on her way to the main road I followed behind her. This wasn't about playing with her tonight. This was about finding where she laid her pretty little head each night.

I didn't try to maintain a distance. I needed to be near her, so I followed close, confident she wouldn't spot me. I wasn't worried about it, though; she never glanced in her rearview mirror. She wasn't very observant of her surroundings.

As the miles passed with me on her tail, traffic growing sparser the further we got from the Portland city limits, my body stirred. She was so close to me. Not close enough to taste, to smell, to consume, but close enough to entice. Damn, I hadn't been this turned on in too long. It was the excitement of stalking my prey, of her not knowing exactly how close I was. I wanted her, and I would have her. It was just a matter of time.

We traveled outside the bustling surrounding cities of Portland, surprising me when she kept on going. She certainly didn't seem like a country girl. She was much too put together for that. But this was just one more thing for me to learn about her.

We came to a small rural area about twenty miles from her office. It was a small, quiet neighborhood, a cluster of houses in the middle of a farming community as if a developer had decided to start a new town then had given up. Nothing too fancy, about a couple hundred houses surrounded by wheat fields, but allowing plenty of privacy for me to hide while I kept a watch on my girl. It worked for me

Janice pulled her fancy red car into the driveway, and I watched as one beautiful, slender leg at a time stepped from the vehicle. I continued past her house, parking on the street near her neighbor. Between the bushes and trees she'd have no chance of seeing me. I could observe all I wanted.

My mind was turning with ideas. I could take her right here and now. I could push her against the side of her perfectly suitable car and fuck her to within an inch of her life. I could throw my hand over her mouth and drag her inside where there wasn't a chance of getting interrupted. The possibilities were endless. But tonight was about observing her—unless I changed my mind.

Her house sat in shadows making it easy for me to move closer. I watched Janice's lights flick on one at a time as she moved from room to room. Peaking in her windows made me almost giddy. Everything was neat and tidy—each item having its own special place. I could have easily predicted just that from the way she furnished her office. From the bright flowers in the vase on the windowsill to the lawn mowed in perfectly straight lines, she appeared to be a sweet little housewife—a housewife without a husband to cater to.

A small garden shed matched the paint on her house, white trim included. I walked over to it and ran my fingers along the edges, thanking her for such a great hiding place.

What I should do is walk in through her front door, grab her by her delicate throat, throw her ass on the bed, and fuck her like she has never been fucked before. I think that's exactly what she needed. I know it's what she craved. It's why she wore those tight little skirts, why she crossed her legs and leaned in toward me as I spoke of darkness, why she licked her lips as she gazed into my eyes.

Some people hid from monsters, and some sought them out. Janice was a seeker. I had no doubt about it. I could have her anytime I wanted, but I needed to know her inside and out before I committed to this. I liked the anticipation—I liked making us both wait for satisfaction.

A light turned off in the living room and I tensed, wondering what she did next in her nightly routine. I was utterly fascinated. I had to move from the shed as I noticed a light flash across the front lawn. I positioned myself by the conveniently placed elm tree in the corner of her yard. There she was.

She stood at her kitchen counter, gazing up sightlessly through the large window as she washed something in the sink. My cock grew hard as I realized the importance of this moment, of where she was, and what it meant.

The faint sound of music playing could barely be heard as she swayed her hips from side to side while washing dishes. She was at peace, looking more content than I'd ever seen her. There was so much innocence about her. I wondered how long it would take me to wipe that look from her face, how long it would take for shadows to overtake the rainbows she must dream about.

I reached down and squeezed my cock as it pulsed painfully. Her shirt was damp, her nipples poking through her blouse. She turned the sink off, her hands resting on the counter on either side of it, giving me the fantasy of how I'd take her the first time. I'd been waiting fifteen years for this moment. As I squeezed to relieve the pressure building, I assured myself I could wait a little longer.

Until this very moment, the timing, the place, *and* the girl hadn't been right. Now I knew beyond a doubt that Janice was the one—the *only* one. She'd help me complete the circle that had started so long ago. She'd allow me to let go of one more memory.

As she gazed at the outside world without being able to see past the reflection in her window, I looked straight into her eyes. It was our moment together. I silently assured her I'd be back, that we'd come together. I took a step forward, lost in the expression of her eyes.

That's when she turned, the lights going off quickly as she made her way to the back of her house. I shook my head as I tried to clear it, not liking what had just happened. Yes, I wanted this connection between us, but it couldn't be so great it overtook me to the point of forgetting who I was.

As she faded away, I turned. I didn't need to follow her anymore. I'd seen all I needed to see. This night had been perfect, had been well worth my wait. We were connected—a connection that couldn't be severed.

The music had finally started . . . and the dance had officially begun . . .

CHAPTER SEVEN

J ANICE LEFT TOWN for two weeks and I grew restless as I waited for her return. We'd lost our momen-
tum because of her conference, and I was angry with
her for interrupting my plans. How dare she not put my
needs ahead of her own.

I told myself to relax, to not let such foolish emotion
into my head, but I was so involved with this girl I didn't
see myself calming anytime soon. It was odd really. Maybe I should simply embrace the emotion.

"I remember the first time I saw her."

My voice reflected nothing about what I was thinking. I looked into Janice's eyes and could see the burning

questions behind her purple gaze. It took several moments for her to turn away from me, and I was quite impressed when she managed to break the spell.

It wouldn't take much for me to have her lying on her back. Our need for each other grew with each visit—especially after we'd been apart for so long. With the emotion this woman was capable of making me feel, I wasn't sure I'd ever let her go.

I leaned forward and allowed her scent to surround me while giving her the pleasure of my body heat to warm her in places I was sure hadn't been warmed in a long time. She tried to hide the quiver, but the electric awareness between the two of us was more than she could handle.

Sitting on the cream colored sofa in the soft-green room, I gazed behind Janice's head while I focused on a hummingbird hovering over a planter dangling from the blossoming cherry tree.

It was just another day in paradise I realized as I consciously shifted my body, knowing Janice was analyzing every little move I made. I truly did enjoy this part of the session with her, actually enjoyed it all, to be perfectly honest. Very rarely was I surprised, and even less often than that were my moves not completely calculated.

Turning my head slowly back to her, I couldn't help but gaze at the pretty brunette with her attention focused on me. I gave her a smile, a look I knew conveyed vulnerability and a need for trust. The barely noticeable hitch to her breath, and the slight lowering of her eyelids, told me she was having the reaction I *needed* her to have.

"We've been sitting here for a while now, Adam," Janice said after I allowed another two minutes to pass without uttering a sound.

I didn't allow her eyes to stray from mine as I leaned more fully toward her. It was all about body language. Each moment of our time together was another puzzle piece slipping easily into place.

"I don't quite know how to begin," I told her with just enough hesitation to have her practically quivering.

"There's not a correct way to begin *or* end," Janice assured me.

I sighed, enjoying the contact of our eyes locked together. She was only free to pull away *if* I allowed it, and right now that wasn't an option.

"I was obsessed with death after witnessing that drowning with my father. Some time passed and I looked for trauma everywhere I turned. If I heard a scream, I'd stop what I was doing, my senses on high alert as I searched for the source of pain. My body would drift in whichever direction the noise had come from. I couldn't stop myself."

I paused again and waited to hear what she had to say about that.

"Go on, Adam. I don't want to interrupt you."

"Do you want to tell me what that means?" I asked.

"No. This is your story to tell. Please trust me to hear it without judging you," she said.

Maybe that was a line all psychologists used. If people wanted to figure it out on their own why did they seek the help of others? I'd asked that question before. I'd never gotten an answer. I never would.

"I saw dead animals on the side of the road, but that didn't appeal to me. I wanted more. In some ways I'd hoped the thoughts would dissipate, but eventually I knew this feeling inside of me was only growing stronger," I told her.

She nodded, her eyes still locked with mine. I could release her gaze, but I chose not to. Janice might as well realize now who held the power between the two of us. If she earned my respect there might not be such a horrific ending for her.

"Who is the 'her' you've been referring to, Adam?" she asked. I'd been waiting for that question. I wanted her eager with anticipation.

"The neighbor girl. I'll never forget the first time I saw her."

"Do you want to describe it to me?" Janice asked. She was trying not to sound too eager, but I felt her blood stir. She could tell this would be a good story, and she didn't want me to close up. I sort of wanted to build the anticipation, but then again I was in the mood to speak of my time with Taylor.

"Her family moved in down the road from mine when I was twelve. It was winter and we didn't see much of them. But then summer hit and neighbors were once again out and about, walking down the long country road, trimming bushes, and clearing garbage from their yards. My dad and I went down to the lake to do some fishing. We went there often, actually, and *she* was there."

"It sounds as if this meant something to you," Janice pointed out.

"She was swimming, and both my dad and I zeroed in on her as she came up out of the water. She was wearing this tiny little pink bikini and I felt an unusual stirring in my body. My dad whistled, but I couldn't turn away from her long enough to see his face."

"How old was she?" Janice asked, her brows knit together the slightest bit.

"Sixteen," I answered.

"And your father whistled?" she asked, still trying to keep her tone neutral. Though she was trying to disguise the disgust, she wasn't doing it well.

"Yeah, he definitely found her attractive, but so did I," I pointed out.

"There's nothing wrong with you finding a sixteen-year-old girl attractive when you're a teenager," Janice said. She didn't add that it was disgusting for my father to feel the same level of attraction, but she didn't need to. I know what people thought.

"From that moment on, I took every chance I could to follow her. I was obsessed with her. She came to our house often that summer, and the next, and I stayed home as much as I could. She and my mother cooked a lot and sat out by the pool. My dad was around more, too, and in a better mood. For so long things had been bad in our house, and then suddenly they were better. It was all because of Taylor."

"Were your parents friends with her entire family or just her?" Janice asked.

"No, just Taylor," I told her. She looked down before she could show me the judgment. I wanted to tell her to hold on, because there was definitely more.

"Did her presence in your life help with the other thoughts you'd been having?" Janice asked.

This was actually a good question. I wanted to pat her on the head—before I grabbed the nape of her neck and pulled that sweet face down into my lap. Between my thoughts of Taylor, and now of Janice, I was incredibly hard. Maybe it was time to fuck this woman. The slight loss of control I felt kept me from doing just that. I wouldn't take her as mine until I could control the situation from beginning to end. That was a rule I never broke.

"No, I was still obsessed with death, but I wasn't acting on it," I told her. "Maybe that was Taylor's influence. I'm really not sure."

"Did anything ever happen between you and Taylor?" Janice asked. I looked down for a moment, giving the illusion that I was either ashamed or unsure of whether to share this or not. I didn't feel either of those things. I just needed to remember to pause every once in a while.

When I looked up, my eyes were clear. I met Janice's gaze, refusing to look away. She shifted before being the first to break the connection. I watched as she subtly took a sweep of my body before looking at the notepad she hadn't touched since we'd begun.

Yes, it was more than time to fuck this woman, more than time to give her what she so desperately needed. Maybe it would be tonight. Maybe it would be tomorrow. I'd have to think about that. My session was almost up, though, and I had to finish my story.

"No, I was never with Taylor," I said before smiling. She seemed confused. She hadn't expected that answer.

"Why did she have such an impact on you?" she asked.

I smiled again. I wouldn't sugarcoat anything now. It had far more impact when I simply spit it out.

"Because I watched as my father fucked her in her kitchen where she could clearly see my mother across the field, working in the yard," I said with no inflection in my voice.

Janice's eyes widened before she managed to school her expression. She once again looked down as I'm sure she took a moment to gather her thoughts.

"Do you want to explain?" Janice finally asked.

"Yeah, I guess I do," I told her. I scooted a little closer to the edge of the couch, imagining pulling her over my lap. I wanted to stroke myself as I looked in this woman's eyes and told this particular story. She waited for me to talk.

"There wasn't a single day that went by when I didn't feel the need to catch sight of Taylor. She'd been coming to my house less and less, and I missed her. Beyond that, I was upset with her for abandoning me. As a teen my hormones were raging. At eighteen Taylor was beautiful and had curves I hadn't known existed in real life. With the end of her nearly daily visits, my home life had gone down the tube again. My mother was drinking all the time, and my father was back to being distant and never home."

I was quiet and I noticed Janice's fingers twitched before she stilled them on her leg. Her need to comfort me was growing in intensity. I stood from the couch and began to slowly pace her office. She leaned back on the couch as she kept her eyes on me. I didn't look at her directly while I continued my story.

"My obsession with death came back with a vengeance, and one day I found myself moving toward Taylor's house. She lived nearly half a mile away, but if the

61

fields were empty I could perfectly see her place from mine. That time of the year the fields were definitely empty."

I could almost taste the berries from the water's edge before those fields became full. But that was another time.

"My mother was in the backyard with a drink in one hand and a cigarette in the other. She didn't even bother to look at me as I passed by. I didn't care anymore. She'd been a different person when I was young and then she'd become a bitch from hell, but for nearly a year she'd almost morphed back into the old mother I knew. She'd given up again, and I didn't have a hope of getting her back. I didn't care to either. She was worthless in my opinion."

"Did that ever change for you?" Janice asked when I again paused for too long.

"No. My mother abandoned me."

"We should talk more on that," Janice said. All therapists wanted to talk about mother issues. It was so damn cliché it was pathetic, and I lost more respect for Janice in that moment. I ignored her suggestion and continued my story.

"I had no clue what I was planning on doing when I reached Taylor's house, but anger and boredom weren't a great combination for me. Her parents' cars weren't in the driveway, and I knew they didn't park them in the garage because it was as cluttered as mine was. However, Taylor's little Ford Escort was sitting to the side of the house and I felt my heart pick up its beat as I quietly drew closer. I snuck through the trees at the back of her property and tried to see in through the windows, but there was no sign of movement."

I walked to Janice's window and looked outside. She gave me a moment, thinking I was emotional at this point, and I let her believe that. It was all part of the game. Finally she stood and moved closer to me, but still kept a respectable distance.

"Is this too difficult for you to speak about?" Janice asked.

I turned, my gaze boring into hers. She took half a step back as her breath hitched in her throat.

"No. Not with you," I told her as I took one step in her direction. She looked as if she was unsure what she should do. But I took immediate pleasure in the fact that she didn't pull away. She was standing her ground. Good for her. I continued my story as I watched Janice's reaction.

"Maybe Taylor was in bed. That thought appealed to me in a big way. I tried the back door and found it unlocked so I quietly slipped inside, then I was still as I tried to listen for any sound of life within the house. There was nothing. I took off my shoes and gripped them in my steady fingers as I slowly made my way through the house.

"I was all the way to the kitchen before I heard voices. I quickly hid behind a door that gave me a clear view of most of the kitchen. Taylor was standing at the sink, but she wasn't alone . . ."

I gave a long pause as I watched Janice's reaction.

"Who was with her?" Janice asked. Though she was asking, she knew. Of course she knew. There'd been no doubt about this from the moment I'd begun this story.

"My father was with her and what they were doing most definitely had nothing to do with cleaning," I said.

"Did you leave?" Janice asked.

I took another step closer to Janice, and this time she did retreat, but her movement was slow as if she wanted to be caught. We danced this way all the way to the wall at the back of her office. I towered over her, not touching her, but letting her feel my presence.

"No, Janice, I stayed behind that door and watched every single moment of it," I said, making sure there was a low growl in my voice.

Her breasts rose, and though I wasn't in complete control of myself, I broke my own rules and lowered my head. I needed to taste Janice's lips—and I needed to do it now with Taylor's image still there between us.

There was only a fraction of a second of protest from Janice as our mouths connected, and then she sighed against my lips and allowed the kiss to consume her. I could lift her sweet ass into the air right now and plunge inside her, but that wasn't how I wanted to take her.

Surprised with the reluctance I felt, I pulled away from Janice, noting her flushed cheeks, her swollen lips, and her glazed eyes. She leaned against the wall, looking shocked at what she'd allowed.

"I think our counseling session needs to continue at your place tomorrow evening," I said in my most seductive tone.

"That's not appropriate at all," Janice told me, but there was no force behind the words.

"Then I guess we're going to break the rules," I said.

Before she was able to say anything else, I turned and walked from the room. She didn't bother asking me how I knew where she lived. She didn't tell me not to come to her. As a matter of fact, her eyes had begged for my touch. It was almost too easy—*almost* being the key word.

I flashed her face through my mind again along with her look of excitement as I'd pulled back from her. That filled me with pleasure I couldn't possibly feel without seeing it on her face. She truly didn't understand who I was or what she was dealing with. It was most definitely time for me to show her.

CHAPTER EIGHT

A S I WAS lying in bed late on this stormy night thinking about all the things I wanted to do with Janice, I couldn't help but remember the night my father was ripped away from me. It was a night just like this one—thunder booming overhead, rain pouring down, and a night so black it was difficult to see my hand in front of my face, let alone anything else.

Lying there stiffly, I remember pulling the covers over the top of my head and wanting someone to protect me from the storm, from the things that go bump in the night. I was too old to think that way, but bad things—irreversible things—tended to happen when nature lost its temper.

Between the cracks of thunder high in the sky, I heard a car pull into our driveway. I nearly sobbed with relief when I realized my mother was home. She was supposed to be gone for three days visiting with my sick grand-mother, but I didn't want to question why she was back early. I just wanted her to hold me until the storm passed. I didn't care at that moment if she hadn't been a good mother in a long time.

I continued to lie there and wait, needing to see her, but not wanting to be busted by my father. If he knew how scared I was about the storm, he'd make me sit in the dark to face my fears. It was best not to show him this weakness. My mother surely would come in to check on me on a night like this. When my grandmother had gotten sick, she'd stopped drinking, had tried to pull her-self together. I hoped tonight was a good night for her—I needed it to be.

When I heard the front door open and I waited impa-tiently for what seemed like hours, I realized she might not come to see me. She might be too tired.

Another crack of thunder literally shook the house with the power of its nearness and I couldn't help but let out a small whimper of fear. I quickly covered my mouth to keep my father from somehow hearing such weakness.

I lay still in bed and listened as hard as I possibly could to the sounds of the creaky house. I didn't hear footsteps, but then again, it was difficult to hear anything beyond the pounding rain and howling wind.

More minutes passed, and still my mother didn't come to me. It sounded like a door slammed inside the house and then another was possibly wrenched open so hard it hit the wall behind it, but that made no sense. Maybe I wasn't able to distinguish sounds anymore with the growing storm.

I closed my eyes and tried to convince myself to go back to sleep. I knew if I was somehow able to let go, when I woke in the morning it would be over. Even if the thunder managed to stick around, it wasn't nearly as terrifying in the morning light.

I was nowhere near drifting off when a scream echoed through our large home. Chills ran up my spine, making the hair on the back of my neck stick straight out as I froze in place. I tried telling myself it was a figment of my imagination, but I next heard a loud explosion.

My ears began ringing and though I tried telling myself it was more thunder, I knew it wasn't. I knew this had happened inside the house. I didn't want to think about what could make that loud of a noise, but I wasn't a baby—I was well aware of the sound a gun made.

As I sat up in bed, I heard the deep roar of a male voice, the words indistinguishable, then came the sound of a female screaming some nonsensical words. What in the world was happening inside my home? Why wasn't my mother or father stopping this? And when were they going to check on me? I shook as I tried to decide what I should do next.

I knew I had to find my parents, but I couldn't seem to crawl from the safety of my bed to do just that. Another roar of thunder boomed outside my window, and before the house stopped shaking there was another roar from the male voice.

I couldn't stay where I was any longer. With reluctance, I climbed from my bed and walked to my door, peering out into the hallway. Another shout echoed toward me before the sound was muffled.

The noise was coming from my parents' bedroom and the door was wide open. My mother yelled something and I was even more confused. It had been a while since I'd heard that tone in her voice.

One foot in front of the other, I crept in the direction of their bedroom. My body was shaking with terror at what I might find. I felt like curling up in a ball in a dark corner and covering my ears, pretending this wasn't happening. Somehow I managed to keep moving forward. I had to know what was happening.

Though it seemed like hours, it took less than a minute for me to reach the bedroom. I stood against the wall, and the sound of my mother's voice was more than clear to me, even if her words were still garbled.

I'd never heard my father cry before. It was an unfamiliar and awkward sound. But as I leaned on the edge of the door, still too afraid to look inside, I realized the sobs I heard coming from the bedroom were coming from a man—most likely my father.

Placing my hand on the doorknob, I tried to gain the courage to peek around the door. The next scream I heard shook my body so hard I didn't know how they didn't hear my whimper. My teeth were chattering together to the point I might lose some of them. Maybe I wasn't as brave as I had thought. Maybe my dad was right about me and I was a coward. I tried to be better for him, to make him proud.

With that thought in mind, I peeked my head around the corner. And then I truly wished I hadn't . . . for many, many years to come.

I woke up and wiped the sleep from my eyes, confusion swirling inside me as I slowly managed to pull myself from the dream of that night so long ago. What was happening to me? Why was I dreaming so much of the past?

As the fog of dreams and reality blended together I realized the answer to that. The circles were all completing. As I got closer and closer to wrapping up my past, it made sense that it would haunt me until I fulfilled my destiny.

I knew what needed to be done next. I knew I had to pay Janice a visit. One more circle would be sealed on this night—one more round finished on the Ferris Wheel. As I climbed from bed, I knew what I was feeling was joy. I could get used to this. My transformation was nearly complete.

CHAPTER NINE

JANICE STOOD AT the kitchen sink just as Taylor had so many years earlier. I'd been watching her house for some time, waiting for her to be in this place. This exact scenario was significant. I'd needed to reenact this scene for quite some time.

The right woman hadn't come along until Janice. She had the same hair color, the same eyes, even the same body. She was a few years older than me, just as Taylor had been.

Even though Taylor was no longer a factor, she had been significant in shaping me into who I was today, and I felt a strong stirring for her all these years later, just as I now did for Janice. I couldn't tell you what that was. But it was better than feeling empty. I had to appreciate both women for giving me such a gift.

Janice's hands were sunk deep into the water of her sink as she gazed out her front window. I wondered what she was thinking about. I couldn't see her expression, which I didn't care for, but I could see the tenseness in her shoulders as she repeatedly washed the same plate while staring out at the setting sun.

My cock stirred as I reached down and squeezed it through my jeans. I could strip and quietly walk over to her, rip off her clothes, and fuck her into submission. I could do that with anyone. But this moment was more than that; this moment was about seduction. I *needed* her to want me. That was very important to this scenario— this fantasy.

Surprisingly, some shitty country music played in the background. I would have thought Janice was more cultured than that, maybe listening to opera or some other crap supposed to stimulate the brain. For me, music was different. I didn't need a radio because I created my own harmony with the cries of my victims. It didn't get more sophisticated than that.

I moved forward and took hold of her hips, enjoying the gasp as she dropped the plate she'd been holding, and water splashing up the front of her, soaking her light blue blouse, and giving me an appealing view over her shoulder as her breasts heaved.

"Wh—" Her voice cut off as I said hello. She tried turning around but my hands held her tightly as I pressed against her ass. She was stiff for only a moment before I felt a tremor race through her. She was well aware it was me behind her. Knowing this broke her medical rules and knowing it was wrong, I still knew she wouldn't fight what she was feeling. That made it that much better for both of us.

"I told you I was coming over," I said, making sure my hot breath washed across her ear before I let my tongue trace the curve of it.

"I told you not to," Janice said, making me chuckle as I wrapped my hands around the front of her, gripping her just beneath her breasts while I pressed harder against her, trapping her body between the sink and myself. This made her tremors grow even more apparent. "I don't want you at my place. It's wrong on so many levels I don't even know where to begin." I was quiet as I waited for her to take a breath and finish. She shook as I pressed against her soft ass.

"I want you to leave," she said, her voice quiet and husky.

I laughed. "Liar." I had no problem calling her out. My hands moved, my thumbs pressing against the undersides of her breasts, making her breathing erratic and her heart thunder. I could feel her coming undone, and almost wished she'd try to fight it just a little.

"You have to stop, Adam. It's not appropriate," she said. Her words would be a lot more convincing if she wasn't breathless and her body wasn't melting against mine.

"Neither of us can stop this," I told her. I needed to taste her so I leaned down and swept my tongue along the back of her neck before sinking my teeth into her flesh with just enough pressure to make her more than aware of my presence. She shook even more and I pressed harder into her, most likely keeping her on her feet instead of her melting into a puddle on the kitchen floor. I wasn't humble about my effect on women—particularly this woman—especially right here, right now.

"Adam, we talked about this," she said. It was a valiant effort to keep her integrity in place. Too bad it wouldn't work. And I loved how much it was turning me on.

I slipped my hands over her breasts and squeezed the sensitized flesh, causing a moan to escape her parted lips. Her nipples hardened beneath my touch and I pinched them even harder, making her moan louder as I twisted and pulled.

"My friend is coming over and could walk in at any time," she said. But she wasn't fighting me as she leaned her head back, opening herself more fully to me. I looked out the window as the day faded, dusk taking its place.

A couple walked past on the sidewalk and that only amplified my desire. I silently begged them to look up, to see what was going on barely twenty feet from them, but they passed on by, oblivious to anything around them. Pathetic, truly pathetic.

"I hope she does," I told Janice and felt her stiffen. "She can watch and learn how a woman *should* be pleasured, or she could join us and you can have two people fucking and licking you all over."

"I would never—" Janice said, mortification now mixed with desire.

"Oh, you *would* and you'd scream," I assured her. "It's amazing what a person will do when their desire is at its peak. There are no boundaries because all you can think about is sweet relief, and you'll take it any way you can."

I twisted her nipples hard as I said this and then flipped her around and ripped her soaked shirt off of her.

She gasped as her blue eyes shone, desire and confusion mixing in them. I didn't give her time to think as I bent down and sucked one perfectly pebbled nipple into my mouth and bit down hard, giving her a mixture of pleasure and pain.

She cried out as she spread her thighs and grabbed the back of my head, tugging on my hair, holding me in place over her full breasts. I would let her have control for a few seconds, and then I'd show her exactly how this night was going to finish.

I ran my fingers down her thighs before moving them back up and slipping them beneath the material of her dress and lace panties, feeling how hot and wet she truly was. She might be trying to fight this, but she couldn't hide her body's response to what I was doing.

I tugged my fingers from her slickness and ran them up her stomach, cupping her breasts again and feeling her completely let go. There was no more protest. I had almost wanted the struggle to go on a little longer, but then again, I was hard and needed to fuck, so maybe next time it could be a little rougher. Maybe I'd have to punish her much sooner than I'd been anticipating for what she was making me think and feel, for the loss of control.

"Do you feel that, Janice, do you feel how hungry you are?"

I was losing patience as I tugged off the rest of her clothes. I loved how a woman looked when she was the most vulnerable, when there was nothing to hide the flush of her skin, the pulse of her heart, or the heat of her arousal. This moment was what made sex so fascinating to me. I thrived on the power and control of it all.

I spun Janice around again and lifted her hands, dipping them into the cooling water of the sink as I pressed against her naked ass. Water splashed over the front of her as I shoved against her. I ran my fingers across her wet torso and over her breasts, loving how slick she was. My fingers circled her neck and squeezed.

I could fuck her while ending her life. I thought about it for a moment, but now wasn't the time. I wasn't ready to let this woman go. Besides that, the scenario with my father and his whore hadn't happened that way. This fantasy had to be played out identically, or as close as possible. I was almost to the point of losing control and forgetting why I was here with Janice.

With that thought I reached up and pushed on her upper back, making her bend forward, making her ass stick high in the air, now lining up perfectly with my cock. I quickly shed my own clothes, pulling free so I could slide my slick head down her crack, pausing at her wet entrance.

She cried out when I didn't immediately plunge inside her, and I smiled as I looked out the window and saw a couple of teenage boys riding by on a bike. One of them glanced at her window and turned away before his head whipped back around, his eyes wide as he took in her breasts swaying just above the water, her nipples hard and wet, her mouth open in an oh of pleasure. He crashed into a telephone pole and knocked himself out, blood trickling from his head as his friend rushed to his side, not knowing what had just happened.

Now!

I slammed inside her and she screamed. She was hot and tight and I couldn't stop a groan from escaping my throat. The sound was foreign to me. I enjoyed pleasure, but I rarely lost control enough to allow sound to release. This made me angry and I thrust in and out of her faster and harder with each push, surely bruising her stomach and hips where they hit the counter in front of her.

The sink water splashed over both of us and still I fucked her harder, the floor growing slick, our bodies coated in water, soap, and sweat. I grabbed her hair and held on tight, tugging her head back and bending so I could bite her neck, leaving my mark on her. She loved it, screaming louder with each connection of our bodies.

I moved faster and harder, holding tightly to her hips as water splashed over the front of her. With a scream she tightened around me, locking us together as pleasure flooded her system, wetting her and sending me over the edge as I pushed hard, exploding within her.

I didn't like how much I shook as I leaned against her, surprisingly unwilling to pull from her tight body. I can't remember that happening before. Maybe it was this moment, this fantasy I'd had for a very long time. Whatever it was, I knew I needed to break this thing between us.

I stepped back and refused to think of it as a departure or loss. She was trembling as she faced the sink, water dripping from her flushed body. The sun had disappeared and the kitchen was dim, but every curve of her body was on display, and I felt the slightest of twitches as I realized I wouldn't mind going for a second round.

There was no way I'd allow that for her *or* myself.

She turned and I refused to look down at her full breasts or tight stomach. I focused on her eyes. This was the part I'd been waiting for anyway. This was what I'd truly wanted to see. It only took a few tense moments, and then I watched as shame entered her expression. I smiled.

There was no way for her to take that moment back. A tremble overtook her frame before she grabbed a towel sitting on the counter and tried to cover herself. Maybe it was because her legs were shaking, but she didn't attempt to run quite yet. I looked at her and tried to decide what would come next. I wasn't sure.

I stepped back and leaned against the kitchen island, not at all uncomfortable in my own nudity. My body was muscled and well cared for. I noticed how she tried not to let her gaze wander over me. She wasn't too good at hiding her feelings—her emotions. That was a skill she'd certainly need to improve if she planned on staying in this profession. *If* I decided to let her to live.

"That was unexpected," I told her, not giving away anything I was thinking.

"Adam . . ." She stopped. Obviously she didn't know what to say.

"You know you don't want to talk of regrets," I told her. Even if she tried to say the night had been a mistake, I had felt her fall apart in my arms. She couldn't take that back.

Moving forward, I stood within an inch of her and waited to see her reaction. She tensed as she held up a hand, then took several steps away from me. I allowed her to do that.

"Don't touch me," she said, her tone pleading. She and I both knew if I were to touch her, she'd ignite again, and we'd next try it on her kitchen table. There was desperation in her voice, and that turned me on all over again, my dick instantly hard.

"We've already done it. What does it matter now?" I asked, more curious than anything. Human emotions fascinated me. I truly wanted to dive into some people's brains and know exactly how they worked, and how they came about decisions they seemed to think were right.

"Because this shouldn't have happened," she told me.

"We can't turn the clocks back now," I said. I found myself growing agitated. I really didn't know why. It didn't matter to me if she had regrets. That normally made it all that much better.

"Please leave."

I thought about ignoring her, showing her the consequences of trying to put me in my place, or telling me no. But one of the more appealing things about this woman was that she didn't cower to me. Of course she truly had no idea of who I was when I wasn't giving her a show, but she wasn't a stupid woman. She had to know there was a darkness about me that wasn't explainable. She was either choosing to ignore that, or it excited her. I think it was much more the latter, which made me smile.

Turning away from her I gathered my discarded clothes, noting they were wet, making them more difficult to put on. I heard Janice's feet as she scurried from the room. I allowed her to go.

As I walked from her house, I knew the connection between us was even greater now. I had never chosen someone I didn't feel was right for me, but in her case, it went beyond that. She'd been what I needed. She'd most certainly been the one.

Now I just had to figure out what would come next in our story.

CHAPTER TEN

JANICE MANAGED TO let a week pass without seeing me. For some reason, I didn't fight her. Maybe I was strategizing or maybe I didn't know how our story was going to come to its climax, but either way, I allowed it.

She shifted uncomfortably in front of me as she sat up stiffly in her chair, her legs crossed, her hands in her lap. The first thing I noticed when I came into the room was the snug slacks and loose sweater she wore. It amused me that she would think her modest attire could stop me from fucking her if I wanted to.

I gazed at her long enough that she had to look away.

"I don't understand why you're fighting me on assigning you a new psychologist," she told me.

"I can destroy your career if you refuse to see me," I reminded her.

She glared at me, and I enjoyed the fire in her eyes. I purposely reached down and grabbed my cock, squeezing it through my pants, letting her see how thick and hard I was at her primness.

"Stop," she told me, looking on the verge of tears.

"Why don't you just drop to your knees and get me off with that pretty little mouth of yours?" I said, my voice pleasant. I undid the top button of my pants and her gaze widened.

"I won't do this, Adam," she said, her spine stiff.

I turned my head and looked at her in a new light. I was slightly disappointed at her not dropping to her knees, a sight I most certainly would love to witness, but her attitude was even more of a turn on so I let it pass.

I unhanded myself and leaned back, enjoying the throb between my legs. I smiled at her and waited. She glared at me. Not very professional, but certainly amusing.

"What are we supposed to be talking about, doc?" I asked.

My shift in topic obviously surprised her. It took a moment for her to regain her composure. I enjoyed that too.

Then I watched as she masked her face better than I'd ever seen her do before, and looked at me with professional eyes that had my dick twitching again. Damn, how I wanted to bend her over the back of the couch I was sitting on. Mmm.

She stopped those thoughts with her next words.

"I think it's time to speak about what happened with your mother," she said.

I looked away from her when she spoke those words. I knew she was expecting a reaction, and though I was good at faking emotion, when it came to my mother there was no faking. It was one part of my life I hadn't mastered up to this point. And if we were back in game-mode I had to play the best I could.

"I don't see why we need to discuss my mother," I told her. Those words were all part of the game. I knew I needed to tell my story.

What was strange was I found I didn't really want to speak of my mother. I wanted to talk more of my father actually. Not because any of it was tragic for me, but because I felt my mother was no one's business. Our last night together was no one's business. It was personal.

"If you aren't ready, I understand, but I think it would be good for you to get it out," she told me. Normally there was a compassionate edge to her voice as she said this sort of thing, but not this time. Now there was too much resentment.

I looked at her, trying to decide what I was feeling or thinking. I wasn't quite sure. I stared at her as I analyzed exactly what it was I wanted to do. There were moments I wanted to slice her neck, and I most certainly wanted to fuck her over and over again, but I didn't understand my reasoning in keeping her alive.

"Do you believe all people have issues with the way they were raised?" I asked her as I thought about my childhood.

She opened her mouth to speak and then slowly took her bottom lip into her mouth and pressed her teeth into it as she often did when she was deep in thought. The little quirks of people were so obvious to spot if you studied them long enough.

"I believe we're all justified in the way we feel about ourselves, other people, and situations," she said in a cookie cutter answer that told me nothing about her as a person.

"I don't believe you," I boldly stated.

Her eyes widened in surprise. I didn't normally call her out on her bullshit answers, but if she wanted to delve into my inner-psyche, then she could give a little of herself as well. She paused a while and then shifted, and I knew I'd won our little battle of wills.

"Okay, I do believe that and it's perfectly okay for you to disagree," she said before a subtle sigh escaped her shiny pink lips. "I also think we're traumatized from the moment of birth."

I waited and she didn't expand. Interesting.

"Now it's your turn to go on," I told her, my lips quirking at the corners the slightest bit. This was fun.

"We're all safe and warm in a cocoon that cushions us from all the dangers of the world. We've got the steady heartbeat of our mothers to comfort us, a constant stream of nutrition to help us grow, and plenty of room to become who we're supposed to be. Then all of the sudden that safe place starts squeezing us, giving us no choice but to leave. We fight it, struggle to stay exactly where we're at, but our safety is gone and we're forced out. We're squeezed through this painful tunnel and thrown into the real world where some person grabs us roughly, slaps us on the back and sticks contraptions into our mouths, noses, and ears. The cord that nourished us so lovingly is ripped from our bodies and the heartbeat that comforted us is no longer beating steadily. Our first sound is a scream."

I replayed her words a couple of times as I looked at her. She shifted again, pulling farther away from me as if she was shocked she'd said so much. But I liked her words. As a matter of fact, I liked them a lot. That was something I hadn't ever considered. Janice was impressing me—not easy to do.

"Maybe that's why nobody remembers their birth," I suggested.

"There have been studies done where people say they do remember," she pointed out.

"I think that's people seeking attention," I told her.

"I believe anything is possible." She was forgetting she was a psychologist and I was her patient. She was forgetting to hate me. We were having a real conversation. I wanted to keep it going, but I saw the moment she realized what was happening and quickly shifted back into client/patient mode.

"Tell me about your mother," she said again, her voice shaky as she tried to regain her professionalism.

Should I give this to her? I wasn't sure. Maybe I would. Maybe I'd tell her my story. Suddenly I began, and I knew once I started, our ending was set. I was almost upset about it—*almost*, since I refused to ever feel regret.

"I decided to go home and see my mother," I began. "I hadn't been there in over five years."

"Why is that?" she asked.

"We didn't have a normal relationship," I told her.

"What do you define as normal?" she pressed.

"I guess that's a good point to make. What is normal?" I replied with a fake chuckle. I didn't feel the merriment of the sound.

"Everyone has their own normal. It's important to remember that," she assured me. Now she was using her sympathetic voice as she let go of our intimacy and focused again on being a counselor.

"Do all mothers tell their children they thought about killing them from the second they were conceived?" I asked.

She didn't seem surprised, but she also couldn't hide her sadness at my statement.

"Unfortunately I hear things like that a lot in my line of work."

"Trust me, I know there are others out there like me," I said. I wasn't interested in bonding with any of them.

"What sort of things did your mother say to you to cause this level of distance?" she asked.

Was I distant? I didn't think so. I was analytical, and I didn't react first and think later. I always thought. I also didn't blame my mother for who I was. If anything I thanked her. I wasn't insecure or afraid. I was strong, getting bolder day by day.

"I asked her once how she'd planned on killing me. She told me she had many versions including abortion, and how she'd fantasized about pushing my head beneath the water while I bathed, about how she had wanted to throw me from a balcony or over the side of the bridge like I was nothing more than an unwanted puppy someone tossed away."

"Did she ever describe it for you, or were those words spoken when she was upset? It seems your mother might have been bi-polar since she switched back and forth from loving and kind, to this other cruel person capable of such venom," Janice asked.

"Oh yes, I'm sure she was. And yes, she went into great detail about my death," I said. I didn't add that I'd carried out a few of her creative methods through the years.

"Would you like to talk about that?"

"The one she repeated the most was drowning. She had a clear fascination of the water. Maybe that's why I was so intrigued when I saw that young kid drown. She did hold my head beneath the surface a few times. I was too young to remember. My earliest memories don't include her in the bathroom with me."

We both were silent for several moments; I sat back and waited. As soon as I spoke those words about my mother's behavior I was over it. I wouldn't dwell on things of the past.

"Tell me about the visit with your mom," she said after several drawn out moments.

There was no point in continuing to hedge on this matter now.

"As soon as I walked in the door I knew something was different, knew there was a shift in the air. I hadn't even seen her yet, but I knew," I said.

I could tell the intensity in my eyes was getting to Janice, but that just made this that much better. She wanted my story, so she was going to get to see a little bit of my dark side. Not all of it. A normal person couldn't handle that, but I knew this woman could handle more than most.

"Your intuition was trying to warn you," she said.

"Yes, and I realized it was time for us to talk about the past, to talk about when my father died."

This surprised Janice. "Did your mother have something to do with your father's death?"

I didn't glance away from Janice as I smiled. I'd been waiting a long time to tell this story. It was drawing closer to the time I'd tell it. She seemed to shrink before me as if she knew she didn't want to hear what I had to say, as if she knew that once she heard it there would be no turning back.

She looked over at the clock and I saw the relief on her face.

"Shall we continue this later?" I asked.

For a moment I wondered if she was going to fight past her fears but then I saw her shoulders droop. At least she'd given herself a little more time. I was almost glad about that.

I wasn't quite ready to let her go. Not quite ready . . .

CHAPTER ELEVEN

J ANICE AND I sat in her favorite coffee shop at one
of the tables on the back patio as we sipped our drinks
and she munched on a peanut butter cookie. I'd insisted on coming here. If she wanted this story I wasn't giving it to her in her dingy, pathetic office.

She'd finally earned the right to this, and I realized she
could take it. But I also was reluctant to give it to her
because I knew once I did our time was that much closer
to ending. It made me slightly gloomy, if that were at all
possible.

"I didn't want to push open the door to my parents' room because I knew the moment I did I was going to see something I didn't want to see," I told her.

"What do you mean by that, Adam?" Janice asked. She forgot to keep eating her cookie as she focused intensely on me.

"I knew how the sound of pain echoed through a house, how a fist slamming into a face crunched. I knew the marks the human body could produce, and I also knew they could be hidden. My father often disciplined my mother—but she'd deserved it."

Janice looked at me as if I'd lost my mind. I smiled at her. "No person deserves abuse, whether it's a woman or a man," she told me.

She spoke those words so passionately I wondered if something had happened to her as a child. I might never find out as our time was running out faster than I'd anticipated. With all things that brought pleasure, pain was right behind. Janice would soon be receiving both pleasure and pain in a much more intense way than she could have ever imagined.

"I finally looked inside and what I saw was far worse than what had been in my head. Taylor was lying over my father, blood pouring from her head, making her hair all sticky and soaking her pale, naked skin. My dad's arms were tied to the headboard, and there was tape across his mouth. Several places on his body were oozing blood. I saw a shotgun resting at the foot of the bed, and every few seconds my father would look down and see it, his eyes filled with fear and tears. I'd never seen him frightened before, but this naked man looked so weak," I said, anger in my tone.

"Oh, Adam . . ." Janice stopped as she reached for me. I didn't let her take my hand.

"My mother didn't even remotely resemble herself. She was wielding a knife, slicing him all over as she continued to berate him. She ignored Taylor's limp body for the most part, but every once in a while her knife would plunge into the brutalized girl."

"How long did you watch this?" Janice asked.

"Long enough to know exactly how she tortured my father," I said.

"Did you call the cops?" I knew she was trying to flash through her mind to all the newspaper articles of crimes as bad as this.

"No, I just watched, too horrified to do anything. I should have tried to stop my mother but I was terrified. I didn't recognize her. Before her final cut on him—his fatal blow—he looked over to where I stood helplessly by. He didn't try to call to me, but I'll never forget the pleading look in his eyes. He didn't rip them away from me as she stabbed him through the heart. I watched as the light went out, as my father left this earth."

"Oh, Adam . . ." Janice was at a loss for words.

It didn't matter, though. I'd told her my story. I just didn't add how I'd waited for ten years to get my revenge. I had killed my mother in the exact same manner as she had killed my father. She hadn't been caught for her crime—by the law at least—but she *had* paid the ultimate price. That was all the satisfaction I really needed for my final closure with my mother and father.

I said nothing else to Janice, just stood up and walked from the coffee shop. I'd told her more than I'd told any other person on this planet. I don't exactly know why that was. I just know it was what it was.

I walked away as I made plans. Janice was sure to not like them, but she didn't get a choice now, did she? Of course she didn't. Her fate had been set from the moment she'd walked into my hospital room, just as my fate had been set the night of that perfect storm.

I had always thought only bad things happened on a stormy night. Looking back, I now realized that was the best thing that could have happened to me. I was now thankful for who I was.

CHAPTER TWELVE

TONIGHT WOULD MOST certainly come to a crescendo where Janice and I were concerned. Even if I have been ridiculously intrigued by her, all good things must come to an end. I must sever our relationship before I grow bored. At this moment I have a measure of affection for her. It's actually sort of odd.

I've thought about this night since the day she stepped into my hospital room. What a beautiful moment that was. I can still close my eyes and smell her sweet perfume. The thought of controlling her, of completing our journey together, gets me even harder than when I was fucking her against that sink with water splashing against our bodies.

I hadn't known how our time would end when our eyes had first locked together, but now my plan was set, and it was coming together perfectly. I know more about this woman than she could possibly realize, and tonight is our last dance.

Janice is predictable, every day the same routine. I don't understand how she hasn't bored me yet. She puts on the same style of silk nighty each night at nine-fifteen before she moves into her small bathroom and washes her face. She then moves to her full-size bed and sits on the edge while she rubs lotion on her feet for exactly two minutes per foot. She then crawls beneath the covers, always lying on her back as she pulls her down comforter up to her chin, leaving her nightlight on as she closes her eyes, falling asleep within five minutes.

In the morning she rises, showers, and dresses within a half-hour, then goes to her kitchen and has the same black coffee with a splash of vanilla creamer, along with a blueberry muffin, while she gazes out her kitchen window, a shadow in her eyes. She doesn't realize I'm always watching, and in the morning she is far less guarded than through the rest of the day.

She parks her car in the exact same position when she returns home every night. One time I moved her garbage can into the place she always has her car, leaving enough room for her to park on the other side of it.

I sat across the street and waited. She pulled up to the house and paused, half her car hanging out into the street. I couldn't see her face, and that irritated me. When a full sixty seconds passed I rose and changed positions, trying to see into her vehicle. But as I got into position she put the car in park and stepped from it, the rear still in the street, causing traffic to slowly move around her. A black jeep went by and honked, flipping her off. She didn't even notice. She was too consumed with the garbage can.

She didn't look around, simply moved to the can and put it back in the exact same place next to the garage, taking a moment to position it just so before she went back to her car and placed it in her driveway. I was utterly fascinated.

Janice worshiped routine. When it was thrown off, she didn't know how to behave. She most certainly didn't know how to deal with me. She normally had her routine down to the very last detail. Tonight that routine would certainly be shattered.

The thought of her reaction to what would happen tonight had me excited—had my body throbbing. I wanted to see her body quiver, trembling with fear. I wanted to watch her expression as the complexion of her silky skin faded to white. I was the one introducing a new routine into her life, the one bringing her fear unlike anything she could have ever thought possible.

Though my plan was in motion, the minutes dragged slowly by as I waited for her. I knew down to the minute what time she'd be near me: 4:36PM. Normally, I wasn't a slave to anything, including time, but on this afternoon I found myself continuously checking my watch, almost growing anxious. I knew she'd be there, but what if . . . No. There were no ifs. She *would* be there. Our dance had to happen.

Across the street from her office was the quaint little coffee shop where we had met before when I'd insisted on moving from her office in order to speak to her, telling her I was anxious in the small, clinical room. I knew this place well.

I strode inside, wanting to make sure to snag one of the small bistro tables positioned perfectly next to the small paned window. It gave me a full view of the busy sidewalk and the creaky front door she'd soon step through.

I needed to see the look of relief in her eyes, knowing her day was over and it was time to order her non-fat vanilla latte and peanut butter cookie. Though she had no idea, this would be the last time she'd wear that look—the last time she'd relax before this night began.

Because today was Thursday she'd pick up her coffee, and delicately nibble on the cookie while walking across the street to the corner market to pick up a gallon of peppermint ice cream. On Friday she'd get to the coffee shop at 5:20 because she'd first take a run in the office gym to make up for the ice cream she would consume over the weekend.

Predictable.

Boring.

Unsurprising.

And oddly . . . appealing.

Ah, 4:35PM. She was a minute early as she practically slid through the old coffee shop door, not a care in the world showing on her face. She'd had an easier day than normal—she hadn't met with me—a bonus in her favor. She was always flustered after our sessions. If I were honest, so was I.

Taking in her face, her body, her movements made the hair on the back of my neck rise. Her easy grace had several men turning to watch her, their gazes momentarily mesmerized. I almost knew how they felt. Almost.

Her smile seemed to turn many people's days from bad to good. I enjoyed watching her, and even more than that, I enjoyed watching how she affected those around her. She got her coffee and cookie and didn't notice me sitting so close. I knew she wouldn't. She was focused, not aware of anything around her.

She moved outside and only briefly glanced in both directions before crossing the street. That was my cue to rise, to start our dance. She stepped inside the corner market as I made it out to the sidewalk. The sun was beginning to set, letting darkness overtake the seemingly innocent neighborhood, giving me the cover I desired.

I took my time walking to my vehicle, safely tucked away two blocks down the street. I changed from my faded blue jeans and white T-shirt to a pair of black slacks and an even blacker sweatshirt. I most certainly wanted her to know it was me, but not until *I* was ready—not until the game was almost over.

At exactly ten minutes from the time she'd left the coffee shop, I began my drive to the country road where she drove home at the exact speed limit each night. The area she drove through was sparse without a neighbor in sight and no one within screaming distance.

It didn't take me long to pull my nondescript car onto a dark gravel road surrounded by nothing but thick rows of blooming corn. There was something almost magical about a cornfield. I was all about the symbolism, after all. The air was pure now that we were outside of the city limits, and darkness had fallen, a full moon offered enough light to give shadows and only those who knew what to look for would see something was amiss.

I positioned myself behind the tree I'd already scoped out, and I placed my father's rifle on my shoulder, looking through the scope, the crosshairs a beautiful image before my eyes. I got one shot at this, and I had no doubt I'd hit my target. The moon shone down on the straight stretch of road, giving me the perfect spotlight for my sweet little Janice. It was her debut, after all, and every star needed her moment on center stage.

In the distance I could hear the sweet purr of the engine of her candy-apple red Lexus. Soon she'd turn the corner, soon she'd be with me. The wait had seemed to take forever, yet it felt as if time had passed too quickly between us. Though I sometimes was sad to see my time end with a woman, I also grew excited at the prospect of finding my new dance partner.

A smile turned my lips up as I saw Janice's headlights lead the way before she came around the corner, the wind blowing the bushes on the side of the road toward her, as if they were reaching for her tires, possibly trying to warn her of what was to come.

The rifle was clutched tightly in my hand, the barrel aimed at the road where the moon shone so brightly. Reaching with my free hand, I tugged the hood of my sweatshirt over my head, giving me more shadows to fade into. I didn't move so much as a toe as I waited, my heart thundering, my body hard, my mind alert.

As her car reached the straight stretch, her lights flashed across me and I smiled. The engine of her car revved as she sped up, her car swerving to the left, letting me know she'd spotted me. The chances of her seeing me had been fifty/fifty. I was glad she had; it was so much more intimate that way.

My only regret was not being able to see her face, which was surely filled with the kind of fear only a targeted prey could testify to. I waited a few more seconds as I aimed my rifle at her sleek car. There was no hesitation as I pulled the trigger.

I hadn't bothered to muffle the sound this time, and the shot echoed through the corn before shattering the glass at the rear of her vehicle, adding more music to my symphony. I hadn't been sure of what would come after the shot, but it was better than I could have imagined.

The car went into a spin as she jerked her steering wheel. She swerved from side to side on the road, and almost managed to right herself before her back tire caught the loose gravel across the white line. Then it was over. Her vehicle spun, diving into the ditch at top speed, and then flipped over onto the hood, a satisfying crunch echoing in the otherwise silent night.

I watched in fascination as her back tires continued spinning while they stood high in the air. Even the crickets couldn't be heard as the wheels gave their last rotation and then the engine died. Was she dead? Was this over?

It was odd, but I didn't know how I felt about that. There was a stirring of excitement within me at this final chapter in my life with Janice, but also a moment of loss. I gazed at the car, searching for movement. Was she suffering? Was she bloody? Was she the same woman?

Unable to wait any longer, I tossed my gun in my car and ran across the road and down into the ditch. Chills rushed through me as my fingers tingled with the need to touch her. I took my time approaching, not wanting to rush this moment.

The blinking red light on the back of her vehicle was almost hypnotic as I took those final steps to her car. It was darker here in the shadows, the moonlight not quite reaching us. I liked it though. It added to this beautiful atmosphere.

I heard the slightest noise and a smile lit my lips. As I glanced inside, I saw movement. My heart thundered in a way I hadn't felt it do before. Janice was a fighter—she wasn't dead.

I stopped and watched as the noise increased, as the movement grew more obvious. Damn! She had certainly been the right choice for me. She was strong enough to be my mate—my victim—my prey.

I wanted to crawl into the car beside her, feel her pain and fear run through me. We were connected in a way that wasn't explainable in an earthly manner. But I wanted a soul mate, and as intimate as the connection between us was, it wasn't quite otherworldly.

As I stood there contemplating what would come next, my eyes adjusted to the dark night sky and her image became clearer. She was struggling to open the driver's door. Her movements were halting, and it appeared there was blood coating her skin, but I couldn't see exactly where it was coming from.

Finally though, she managed to get the door open. The light came on as she pushed through the broken glass, crawling on her hands and knees, coming closer to me. Her cries were muffled, and blood dripped from her mouth and nose.

I examined her without her seeing me; it was obvious her shoulder was broken, and she might have a punctured lung by the sound of her breathing. Her cries were weak and she didn't seem to have the energy to get away from the vehicle. But once again her strength prevailed.

When she was free of most of the glass, she fell down on her side, then attempted to sit up. She failed. A whimper escaped her, and she flopped back, her eyes closed. I waited. Anticipation built without me so much as blinking.

This time she was the helpless one, and I was standing above her. The symmetry of our situation coming full circle didn't fail to grab my attention. No, this wasn't a hospital bed, and of course I wasn't a doctor, but still, she was lying helplessly before me, and I was the one who was strong.

Electricity filled the air. Nature itself was practically buzzing. I made the slightest of noises and she stiffened. She'd thought the danger was over, forgetting about the gunshot that had made her crash in the first place. Tilting her head in my direction ever so slowly, her eyes finally met mine.

It was the most erotic sensation I've ever felt. Pain was radiating off of her in waves, and we were both silent as we stared at one another. She opened her mouth, then closed it as more tears fell. She didn't look away from me, and she didn't tremble in terror. She seemed to know her fate, accept it even.

Oddly this aroused me more. I couldn't end her life like this, not with her lying so helplessly on the ground. She'd been a worthy opponent and had earned a touch of my respect. I smiled at her as I knelt down. I didn't try to refrain from touching her. My fingers swept along her cheek and she flinched, but she didn't turn away.

"Just do it," she said, her voice trembling. "It's been your plan all along, so do it." There was fire in her eyes as she glared at me. The effect was ruined with the swelling of her cheek.

I didn't try to hurt her further. It was actually quite fascinating. Why didn't I want to finish this right now? Slowly the anger drained from her eyes and pain returned, along with more tears. She lifted a hand as if to reach for me, but she was too weak to do even that much.

"My sweet little Janice," I began. I leaned down and pressed my lips against hers before running my tongue along her jaw. Ah, she tasted sweet.

A shudder passed through her. She might want to think it was revulsion, but there was more than just love and hate between us. We had a connection, and neither of us could deny it in this surreal moment.

"Your life was supposed to end tonight," I said. I kissed her again and she closed her eyes as she let out ragged breaths. Her body was in too much pain, and she went into shock as she gave in to the darkness reaching for her.

I ran my fingers across her bottom lip and gazed at her for a long moment. Had this woman actually gotten to me? Had she made me feel something so foolish as compassion? That couldn't possibly be.

I was confused as I stood up and loomed over her. I listened for at least thirty seconds, and while her breathing was painful, and blood was obviously in her lungs, she wasn't giving in to the darkness. She was holding on. This thing between us wasn't quite over. Our conclusion was nearing, but it wasn't happening tonight.

I began moving toward my vehicle, not understanding what I was feeling. I knew I'd see her again, there was no doubt about it. I'd see her again *very* soon. She was still mine—mine to do with as I pleased—mine for the taking.

I heard the distant sound of sirens and looked out as if I could see the emergency vehicles coming. How did they know of the wreck? I'd planned all of this down to the minute and there was no one nearby to call 911. A scowl crossed my face as I turned back to gaze at her broken vehicle. I hadn't purchased a new car in years because of the technology, the ability to be spied on inside the painted metal walls. The moment her Lexus had lost control, emergency services would have been dispatched. How could I have let such an important detail escape me? It was such an utterly human mistake.

I picked up my pace as I jogged to my piece-of-shit car. I climbed inside the driver's side and jammed the car into reverse as I headed in the same direction as the emergency vehicles. My lights stayed off as I used the moonlight to guide me down the deserted road. Did they want to play chicken with me? I was more than game.

This night hadn't turned out how I'd expected, but that wasn't a bad thing. Sometimes the greatest pleasures in life happened without preparation. I'd planned on her dying, but she'd caught me by surprise.

Things hadn't developed in the order I'd envisioned, but all that meant was I'd see her again soon—very, very soon. My fingers clenched on the steering wheel as I imagined the next time our eyes met. When she gazed at me, would it be the last time?

We'd soon find out.

CHAPTER THIRTEEN
Janice's POV

I T WAS ODD how much pain the human body could endure. It reached a point where it was almost interesting. At first I couldn't pinpoint where I hurt because it seemed there wasn't a single inch of me that didn't feel as if I were being stabbed over and over again.

I'm not exactly sure what happened. One moment I was driving, enjoying the country ballad on my radio station, and then I'd noticed that shadow. It had caught me by surprise, seeing a dark figure standing against a tree, not even trying to keep hidden. Had he been holding a gun? It appeared as if my headlights had glinted off the long silver barrel of a weapon. It happened so quickly I couldn't be sure.

Then my window shattered and I'd felt an odd sensation in my back. The noise startled me, and I made such a foolish mistake. I tugged on the wheel and lost control of my vehicle. I nearly got it back when my tires hit the loose gravel on the side of the road.

I've heard people say it feels as if they are going in slow motion when they are in a terrifying situation. I'd counseled many people, speaking on this very subject. I hadn't ever experienced anything like it until right then. But they were right. It had felt like I was barely moving, as if I should have been able to stop whatever was happening.

But the pause in time didn't last long. Soon my car flipped over and I must not have latched my seatbelt properly because I was thrown forward, my head slamming against the windshield before my body was wrenched backward. The next thing I knew I was on the roof of my car, surrounded by glass, my blinker still clicking in a hypnotizing way.

I hurt all over. I remember reading once that someone said if you could feel pain, you should be grateful because that meant you were still alive. Obviously the person who'd said it hadn't ever felt anything like what I was experiencing. Or maybe, and far more likely, I just wasn't as strong as I'd always believed I was.

Somehow I managed to crawl from the vehicle, hearing the sound of my painful whimpers. It was almost reassuring how the sound broke up the otherwise eerie quiet of this surreal night.

I moved, almost feeling as if it wasn't my body crawling along the ground, as if it wasn't my blood spilling. The pain began to have an odd affect. I wasn't feeling it through my entire body anymore; it was now pulsing in certain areas. It wasn't growing worse, but again, it almost felt as if it were being described to me by someone else—as if it were happening to someone else.

Maybe this was the power of the brain. Right now I wasn't in good shape, and though I didn't know how to process what was happening to my body, my brain was protecting me. I tried sitting up and failed. Lying back, I closed my eyes. If I allowed myself to pass out, then I wouldn't feel any more pain.

That's what I'd do. I'd simply take a nap and when I woke everything would be so much better. I felt myself drifting away when a noise alerted me that something else was wrong.

Though it sent a shock of pain through me, my body stiffened. I'd forgotten about the man who'd been standing in the shadows. I'd forgotten why the crash had happened in the first place. There was only so much a person could process when their world was crumbling around them.

I didn't want to face whatever was out there, but I wasn't a person who would bury my head beneath the sand. If I was about to die then I wanted to look my attacker in the eye, wanted them to know they wouldn't break me—mentally at least.

When my eyes locked with *his* I gazed at him in disbelief. I don't know why, but I wasn't expecting it to be Adam standing before me, his face shadowed by the black hood he wore. I almost smiled at how foolish I'd been. How could I have thought it could be anyone else? Was I truly that naïve? Had I failed that much as a woman *and* a psychiatrist?

Anger overtook the pain I felt. It was still there, but I pushed it to the back of my mind. From the moment I'd stepped foot into this man's hospital room, he'd been playing with me, and I'd allowed him to do it. I'd allowed him to compromise me in so many ways. How had I been so unaware of the monster he was?

My frustration and pain led to more tears falling and a renewed sense of rage. He was going to kill me—that much I knew. I could see it in his eyes. But I'd be damned if he'd see me beg, if my last moments on this earth would be me pleading for my life.

Though terror consumed me from the inside out, it didn't matter. I'd made the choices in life that had led me to this exact place. I'd played it safe from the time I'd been old enough to know right from wrong, had always been the good girl, always followed the rules. With Adam, I'd come unwound. And though I wouldn't admit it to another living soul, I'd enjoyed it.

How odd that the first time I break the rules is going to cost me my life. It wasn't quite computing in my brain. My legs had gone numb, but I didn't stir in front of Adam. I didn't want him to know there wasn't a chance of me running. What good would it do me anyway? Even if I had the full use of my body, he was stronger, and obviously smarter, because here we were.

He knelt down beside me, a smile on his lips. When he reached out and ran a finger across my sore cheek I tried to pull from him, not wanting to feel anything but disgust and anger toward this man. I glared at him, still not turning away as his finger lingered on my jaw.

"Just do it," I told him, hating the weakness in my voice. "It's been your plan all along, so do it." The last of my words ended on a sigh, but even if I was weak, I still had a spark of fire running inside me. I told him how deeply my hatred ran with nothing more than a condemning look.

When his own gaze softened the slightest bit, I was so shocked I lost the ability to hold on to my anger. With the loss of my rage, my pain returned ten-fold. It was nearly unbearable now. I foolishly reached out to Adam, silently pleading with him for help. It was a foolish gesture, only happening because of how pathetic I was, but I couldn't hold up my arm anyway. I let my hand flop back to the ground without losing my pride.

"My sweet little Janice," he said, and more tears streamed down my cheeks. He was so good at how he spoke, at how he managed to make me feel special. How was that possible? The logical part of my brain knew this man had tried to kill me, that he most likely still would. But with the single utterance of a word of endearment I wanted to reach for him; I wanted him to comfort me.

He leaned down and kissed me, his tongue tracing my lip before running across my jaw. I wanted to hate the gesture, wanted to push him away. Instead, a shudder passed through me, not of desire, but of need, a need to make this all go away, a need to be held through this unimaginable pain.

"Your life was supposed to end tonight," he told me before kissing me again.

I tried to tell him that I knew, tried to tell him again to just do it, but the edges of my vision began to blur. I almost wanted to stay there with him in my final moments, to see his face one last time before I gave in to the blackness, but my eyes were too heavy. I closed them and let go.

When next I woke, it was to the sound of sirens. I saw the flashing lights, but I didn't want to open my eyes. I wanted to stay in the darkness. Someone was speaking to me as a cold disk was pressed to my chest.

"Her pulse is weak," a voice said.

"We're losing her," another offered.

"With these injuries I don't see how she's lasted as long as she has," the first voice quietly whispered, empathy in his tone.

"She's damn strong," the other offered.

I opened my eyes and a young man hovered over me. He seemed surprised before he masked the look and rested his hand on top of mine.

"There you are," he told me with a reassuring smile. "We're going to load you into the ambulance and everything will be just fine."

He was lying. I'd stretched the truth to enough patients in my short time as a psychiatrist to know when a patient was being appeased. I no longer was hurting. Most people would be pleased by that, but now I understood *that saying*, now I *knew* what it meant to need to feel the pain to know you were still alive. I no longer could feel it because my body was shutting down.

I didn't say anything as the two paramedics shifted my body and scooted me onto a bed. Though the young man tried to hide it from me, I saw his glove covered hand coated in blood—in my blood.

Now I knew that pain in my back had been a bullet. It had pierced my lung and come out through the front of me, splitting my seatbelt in half and allowing me to be slammed into the windshield. Adam couldn't have planned a more perfect shot if he'd been trying. He'd gotten lucky, and now I'd die because of it. I was okay with that. I don't know how I was, but I was okay.

I also didn't think he'd be. That gave me a tiny bit of satisfaction. There'd been something about the way he'd looked at me in those last few moments of consciousness. We did have a connection—and now it would be over. Death would free me, but it might bind him even more.

The paramedic seemed so sad I wanted to reach for him, to tell him it would all be okay. I couldn't move my arm so I gave him a smile, or at least I attempted to. I wasn't sure if I was pulling it off.

"It's okay," I said, my voice barely audible.

"Hey, that's my job to say," he told me, unable to pull off the reassuring smile this time.

"It's okay," I said again, feeling as if I were in a tunnel, as if he was moving farther away from me each time I blinked.

"Don't do this! Don't give up," he yelled. "Come on, don't let go."

His voice faded away until I eventually couldn't hear him at all. I had lost sight of him long before the voice floated away. I don't know where I was, or where I was heading, but it was neither hot nor cold, dark nor light, empty nor full. It was nothing. There was absolutely nothing.

CHAPTER FOURTEEN

AN UNUSUAL SENSE of sorrow washed over me as I continued to drive further away from Janice, but I immediately pushed it down, focusing on the victory of this perfect moment instead.

Not all plans had to work out the way they were expected to, I assured myself. I'd rehearsed this plan in my head over and over again, and this wasn't the outcome I'd expected. But I was more ready than I'd thought for our relationship to end. She had too much pull over me and I couldn't allow that.

Seeing her lying so helplessly as she defiantly looked up at me and challenged me to complete my mission had been fascinating and the most stimulating experience I'd ever felt before. It was pure music added to my symphony entitled *Janice*.

Though I felt the ache of her loss as I drove, I was reassured with the knowledge that I would see her again very soon. Our eyes would once more connect, and the next time we faced each other I wouldn't hesitate to take away the very light that intrigued me so much. She was in no way perfect—and she wasn't my soul mate. She was just a woman, and I would break the bond between us.

My headlights were still off, and I defiantly continued in the direction of the oncoming flashing red lights and sirens. One at a time they sped past me, almost causing me to steer off the road as I craned my neck to watch them. The stimulation was so much more than I was used to. This was different than my other victims, this was magical. I'd never allowed another dance partner to interfere with a kill, but these ambulances were about to do just that. I scowled at the thought.

No more than ten minutes after passing the emergency vehicles, I slowed my car to a stop on the side of the road. I'd walked away from her knowing she was still alive—not something I'd ever done before. I hadn't been able to give her the final blow. And now she had rescuers arriving.

I always liked to spend time with my victims after I'd taken away their very last breath. I loved to caress their lifeless bodies one final time as I thanked them for the honor of becoming my dance partner. If they took her too far from me, I wouldn't get that chance.

I didn't care that she might rat me out, that she might tell these people who I was and what I'd done. They could try to catch me—others had. If they wanted to join the dance, they'd better be prepared for the song. This wasn't a middle school event, and *no one* would go home safely.

Without hesitation, I wrenched my vehicle around and turned back in her direction. This was my girl—my prey—my dance partner and I'd be damned if I allowed anyone to take away our last moments.

I sped down the road as fast as my junker car allowed, turning corner after corner, feeling like she was drawing farther away from me instead of closer. Finally I could see flashing red and blue lights up ahead and I wanted to let out a sigh of relief, but I couldn't *feel* her fear anymore, couldn't *feel* her pain. I shook with the idea of that loss.

I approached the scene with just enough time to see the ambulance door close behind Janice, giving me only a view of her feet. I hadn't gotten to see her beautiful face, raising my anxiety levels even higher. They drove off before I reached them, leaving me no choice other than to follow behind.

My knuckles were tingling and white from gripping the steering wheel tight as I kept a reasonable distance from the ambulance without letting it out of my sight. I had to be with her, had to look into her eyes. The farther the ambulance pulled from me, the more loss I felt, causing sweat to drip down from my forehead—another new sensation for me.

Finally, after what felt like an eternity, I saw the glow of the hospital lights come into view. It was about the most beautiful sight I'd ever witnessed. The ambulance screeched to a halt in the quiet bay area, and I halted my car so I could see them.

The doors blocked Janice from me, and I slammed my fist into the steering wheel in a bout of anger that was completely unlike me. That only made me more enraged that she was affecting me this obviously—this humanly.

Janice was long gone by the time I threw my car into a parking place and jumped out, needing to ensure I didn't miss a single minute more with my dance partner. The hospital was small, and as I rushed inside the doors marked for personnel only, I saw her. The bright lights showed her bloody hands and body.

The doctors stood around her, but no one moved, no one did anything. A tube was hanging from her throat and her skin was pale. Why weren't they trying to help her? No monitors were beeping, no sound other than the quiet voices of the medical staff could be heard. It was eerie and not in a good way.

In shock I watched as a nurse came over and removed the clear tube that had been pushed down her throat. Then much to my horror, the same woman pulled up a sheet and covered her face from my view.

"No!" My voice roared through the corridor, alerting the staff of my presence. All of them looked my way. "She's mine! You won't be the ones to take her."

My rage was fierce and I saw the terror on the nurse's face who'd covered her. She *should* be afraid. I was filled with outrage. How dare she hide Janice from me! I strode toward Janice, not caring who was in my way. I would kill anyone who tried to stop me. This was *my* time with her.

"Get security," the doctor quietly said to one of the nurses. "Hurry," he added with a sense of urgency.

I ignored him, silently telling him he was wise not to touch me. I carried a six-inch blade against my side that I could have out so quickly he wouldn't understand the pain radiating from his throat before he dropped to the ground. I forgot about him as I looked upon the still outline of the body that was Janice. Blood was soaking through the once sterile sheet. It wasn't beautiful at all.

I didn't hesitate any longer as I softly pulled the cotton from her face, gazing into her violet-blue eyes. Reaching out, I softly ran my fingers over the top of her eyelids, closing them for the last time. I leaned down to rest my face against hers before I slid my tongue across her jaw as I'd done that first time.

Her taste and scent would forever stay with me. She was mine, and she'd been taken from me without my permission—without my final blow. I had no choice but to forgive her for this, though, because she was indeed gone. I could feel it, could feel the lost connection between us.

I tuned out the doctor who was urgently speaking into his phone, probably trying to get security to pull themselves away from their coffee and donuts to save his dead patient from a crazy man. I didn't give a fuck. This moment wasn't about them, it was only about Janice and me.

"Thank you," I whispered in her ear. These words were for us alone. "Your song has come to an end."

When I finally was done telling Janice goodbye, I looked up to see terror in the eyes of the people surrounding us. I don't know what my expression offered them, but it was enough to make each of them take a few steps away.

I gazed at them, refusing to allow them to look away, and then I smiled. It was a lifting of the lips that had nothing to do with joy. Today was a sad day, but it wasn't all bad. I could take each of these people out, but I didn't care to. I instead turned and walked back out the way I'd come in.

Tonight hadn't been the victory I'd wanted, but our conclusion had come to a satisfying end anyway. And now, because of that, my dance with Janice has ended, but that just meant a new song was about to begin with someone else . . .

EPILOGUE

WHY IS IT that the world wants a horror story? Why does that story have to get darker to catch people's attention? Why do despair and greed, lies and revenge, sex and pain call to us? The answer is, there is no answer.

Beyond that, these aren't questions I have a desire to find an answer to. They are merely thoughts inside my head. You see, I've now fully accepted who I am and what my purpose in life is all about.

Your first instinct might be to run from me, but you don't need to do that. You aren't in any danger unless you're chosen. I'm not a monster—though many would call me that. Something happened to me in this past year, something I can't explain. I need more. I want more, I expect more. I should be praised because I truly make the world a better place.

Yes, there are monsters, but you might not realize there are certainly more than one kind. Did you honestly think evil could be categorized? Did you believe you were safe tonight when you turned that small, insignificant bolt on your door to the lock position?

If you believe that, you're a fool. Look to your left, and then your right, look forward *and* behind you. Are you getting scared? You should be. You should be very frightened. Because I guarantee you that in one or more of these directions, there are windows. Right now those windows could be lit up, giving you the illusion of thinking all is well in the world. The flowers are blooming, the birds are chirping, and the dog is chasing a ball.

Or it could be storming outside. A little scarier, correct? But still, nothing to give you those goosebumps, that warning of impending danger. The thunder sounds and shakes the house, and you worry that the power might go out, but you still aren't afraid.

But at night, oh, at night. Now, that's an entirely different feeling. You look to those windows, and if you think about it your stomach tightens, your throat closes just a little bit, and saliva fills your mouth.

You can't quit looking at the windows now, can you?

Maybe now there's a little buzzing going on inside your ears, and it feels as if the temperature in the room has dropped several degrees. But again you look. Is the curtain closed? Is there a sliver of black you can see through to the outside? Or are you more like me? Do you like to leave your windows wide open so you can see out—and others can see in? I have nothing to hide. I'm proud of who I am and proud of what I do. You can have a peek inside if you'd like.

Let me share a secret with you. None of it matters. The curtains are an illusion. They offer no protection. Just like that tiny little insignificant piece of metal you think is locking your door gives no safety. That lock can be picked, and that window can be shattered. And those monsters you think you're keeping out? They can come in at any time they want—and they do.

They gaze in your windows, they stand over you while you're asleep, and they reach out for your feet when you step up to your bed. They hide in the corners, and they remind you each and every day that they can get you any time they want. That's the best part—when you're being hunted—when *I'm* hunting you.

Yes, those monsters are real. But what would surprise you is that they aren't who or *what* you think they are. No, those monsters are so much worse than you could ever possibly imagine because they live within you—they *are* you.

My life has always been a Ferris Wheel, just like that moment with my mother and father when I thought that was what normal was supposed to be, we went up and came down, we turned corners and we gripped the safety bar tightly.

But the ride eventually ended. I begged my dad to do it over and over again. He'd smiled indulgently at me and told me not to get too greedy, that all good things must come to an end.

I would have never known that twenty years later those words would flow through my mind, would offer me such insight. I hadn't known then that a moment at a State Fair would be a spotlight in my life.

Janice was taken from me. That wouldn't happen again. We never got to complete our dance and now I was lost. I learned something from her, though. I learned about myself. She'd given me something I hadn't had before—she'd given me emotion.

Don't worry, I'm not a changed man, but now I feel something. I feel a need to connect. I have to change the way I dance through this life. Killing for the sake of purging the world is no longer satisfying for me. No. I need to play a new game. Janice taught me that, and I'll be eternally thankful to her for the valuable lesson.

She hadn't been the dance partner or the soul mate I'd been seeking, but she'd given me the knowledge that someone out there would easily fit that category. I just had to find her.

Luckily for me, I might have done just that.

Sitting in this small coffee shop in a seedier part of Portland, I watch her. I'd spotted her a few weeks past and she'd intrigued me, but in that moment I was still dancing with Janice, and I only allowed one partner at a time.

But Janice was gone now, had left me without my permission. The new dark-haired woman sat in the back of the coffee shop, a slightly beaten up computer resting on the table as her fingers flew across the keyboard.

Her brows were wrinkled the slightest bit as she concentrated deeply on what she was typing. I pictured many scenarios in my head of what she could be doing at two in the afternoon on a weekday when most people were at their boring nine-to-five jobs.

Was she a freelance writer? A stay-at-home mother? Laid off? Was she simply chatting on social media? I didn't know yet because I hadn't allowed myself to get to know her. I had to make sure she was the right person, had to make sure she inspired me to feel . . . anything.

I could follow her from the coffee shop and slit her throat before anyone knew what was happening right in front of them. But that wasn't appealing. Killing was an art, and the act of building a relationship with a victim was a game. Why hadn't I figured this out sooner? Why had it taken losing Janice to know this?

None of that mattered. It was time to move on from Janice. It was time to press forward and develop a new relationship, and luckily for Mona, I'd chosen her. You might think she wasn't lucky, but you'd be wrong. If she was a worthy opponent, we'd have a beautiful relationship—an epic dance.

Who could be unhappy about being challenged? Who would want to stay in a boring rut when they could instead live their life to the fullest? Did it matter that their life might be shortened? I'd rather say I danced than I slept. Wouldn't you?

What I see in Mona is a woman who laughs without mirth, who smiles without joy, who is bored and restless. I see she's searching for something more. I see she *needs* me. I'm willing to help. When she leaves the coffee shop this time, I'll get up and follow her.

Our dance has officially begun . . .

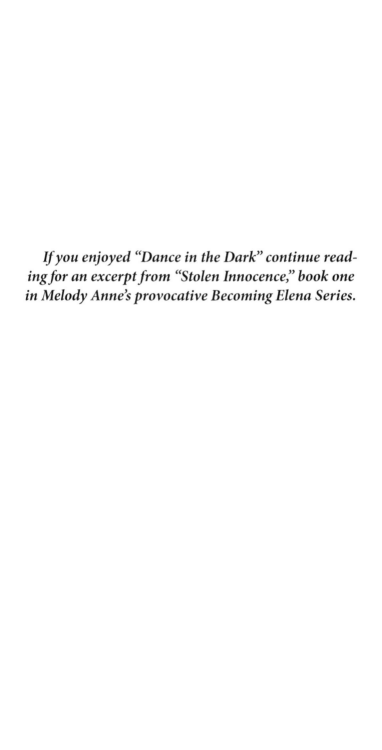

If you enjoyed "Dance in the Dark" continue reading for an excerpt from "Stolen Innocence," book one in Melody Anne's provocative Becoming Elena Series.

Stolen Innocence

Becoming Elena
book one

By

MELODY ANNE

PROLOGUE

FOR FIFTEEN YEARS, Elena's life had been better — had been as close to perfect as she was allowed to have. She'd let go of her past and had embraced her present, had accepted who she was. She'd liked the person she'd become.

It had all been because of *him*.

Now she found herself leaning against the wall, wondering how she was still on her feet. The world was a cruel, cruel place and she had first-hand knowledge of that. Everything had come crashing down around her with no way of fixing it — not this time.

She'd been in love — as much as she was capable of feeling that foreign emotion. Maybe that wasn't what it was. It could very well have been need. But even if it was need, that was so much stronger an emotion than she normally felt. Elena wasn't a fool — she knew to care for anyone was extraordinary. It was even greater to have them care for her. She fell down to the floor, her legs no longer holding her up.

He had been hers for so long she wasn't sure she could live without him. In a ball she laid there. Not too many people knew her story. She'd covered it up well, was respected, owned a business, and had a husband — not that he was worth mentioning.

Those she was closest to would be shocked by her choices in life. They wouldn't care there was a reason she was who she was. They would just hate her — call her a monster — call her a whore. One of the few women she'd actually called *friend* had discovered her most coveted secret this very night — had walked into the room while Elena had been begging her previous lover to take her back.

The woman — her friend — had vanquished her from her life and the life of her son though *he* was a grown man and could have chosen to stay with her. But even if her friend hadn't vanquished her, *his* girlfriend, who claimed to love him, had already done so. The money-greedy bitch. She couldn't love *him* like Elena did. She didn't understand *him* — didn't have a clue how to handle the pain he'd suffered.

Elena had taken his hand, had guided him through his nightmares, had taught him how to deal with them, how to deal with life. She'd been the one to heal him, had been the person there for him when he'd needed it most. She'd held him, whipped him, and made love to him in every conceivable way. And he'd chosen that naïve little girl over her. If it hadn't been for Elena *he* never would have been whole enough to be in a relationship with her. But instead of thanking Elena, the girl had taken *him* away.

That chapter was closed so tightly she would never be able to fix it this time. She couldn't believe she'd lost *him*. She could barely breathe she was so upset.

The pain was too much. It was too much.

Elena had been through hell and back. But through it all, she'd managed to survive. She wasn't sure she'd survive this, though. She'd needed *him* and he'd moved on.

She and *him* had been the perfect match from the moment their eyes had met — both of them filled with so much pain no one else could possibly understand. She'd recognized it in him and she had known she couldn't turn away from what had to be done.

From that moment on the two of them had been one. Elena didn't care if the rest of the world looked down upon their relationship — she had always known it was pure, it was love, it was extraordinary.

But it was over. She had lost *him*. It had all been for nothing. Everything she'd ever done that had led her to this point had been for nothing. Elena hung her head, unmoving as she gave up on it all.

Without *him*, she had no will to carry on.

CHAPTER ONE

Fifteen Years Earlier

S ITTING ON HER little brother's bed, Mary gave Tommy a gentle smile as he bounced up and down in excitement, his hands cupped before him, a huge grin showing the whiteness of his teeth.

"Come on, Sissy, I can't wait," he said with a giggle.

She placed a box in his hands, and his eyes shot open as he looked at the bright green wrapped package with a white satin bow on top.

"What is it?" he asked as his seven-year-old fingers reverently trailed across the ribbon.

"You'll have to open it to find out," she told him with a laugh.

Carefully, unlike most seven-year-olds, he slid the bow off and undid the tape, not wanting to tear the wrapping. She knew he would save it, as he saved all his wrapping. It was an odd habit, but she sort of liked that he did it. It was only one of the many things that made Tommy unique.

When the box was open, he pulled out a journal with a compass and his name etched on the front, with a pencil attached to the side.

"Wow," he said, his fingers rubbing over the raised lettering. "This is my name."

"I know you want action figures and pellet guns, but I wanted to give you something that makes you think of me when I'm away at college," she told him.

"Why do you have to leave?" he asked for about the hundredth time, his eyes swimming with tears.

"I'm going to a university. Besides, this house is too small, and it will be easier on Mom when she's not feeding four mouths."

"Mom loves us both," Tommy insisted.

"Yes, I know she loves me just as much as she loves you, but I'm graduating high school soon and I'll be a grown-up. This is what grown-ups do," she tried to explain. "And see that compass on the front cover? If you put your hand on that and close your eyes and think about me, you will know I'm out there, and I'm thinking about you," she assured him.

"I just don't want you to leave," Tommy said as he carefully set the package down and curled up on her lap, something he'd done since he had been crawling around on the floor as a five-month-old.

Their mother and Mary's stepfather, Dave, both worked full-time, so Mary had always spent a lot of time with her little brother. Sometimes, she was frustrated when she had to babysit instead of going out with her friends, but most of the time she didn't mind. She loved Tommy, even if she hadn't been thrilled when her mother had first married Dave.

It wasn't that Dave was horrible or anything. He was mostly indifferent to her. She would rather have that, than have him come in and try to act like her father. No one could replace her dad; she wouldn't allow it.

He'd died when she was only eight, but she still remembered how he would rush in the door after work and pick her up, giving her a kiss on the forehead before spinning her in a circle. He'd always told her she was the most important person in the world to him. She was his princess.

His death had left her empty. But she and her mother had eventually begun to heal. And then Dave had come into the picture. Mary was glad that Dave made her mom happy, but he drank a lot, and he was lazy, in Mary's humble opinion.

Her mother did everything. Worked full-time, cleaned the house, cooked, came to all of Mary's school functions. When her mother had gotten pregnant with Tommy, Mary had been worried. Because that meant even more changes.

But from the moment her little brother had been born, she'd cherished him. And he'd bonded with Mary. She really did adore the kid.

"You have to come home and see me a lot," Tommy insisted. "Promise me!"

She held up her hand, her pinky sticking out. "I promise."

They locked their pinkies together, and then she leaned forward and kissed his cheek.

A pinkie swear could never be broken. It was the most sacred of oaths in her opinion.

But sometimes, the promise was taken out of a person's hands. Sometimes their feet were swept out from beneath them. And sometimes promises were broken . . .

CHAPTER TWO

THE NOISE WAS driving her insane! Mary loved her little brother — his friends she could do without. And her stepfather insisting she play all the little kid games was making it even worse. She needed freedom, and she needed it now.

Grabbing a rose from the vase of flowers sitting on the dining room table, Mary plucked a petal off and moaned.

"What's the matter?" her mother asked with an indulgent smile.

"I need to get out of here," Mary grumbled.

"I told you I don't like you walking when it's late, especially now with snow on the ground," her mother said, a hand on her hip.

"You also know I have to take a walk each night — rain or shine — or I feel like the walls are closing in on me," Mary countered, gripping the long stem tightly in her fingers.

Her mom sighed as she gave Mary a once-over. Before she said anything, Mary knew the battle was over.

"Don't be out late."

"I won't."

With a roll of her eyes, Mary walked from her front door with a huge sigh of relief. Sometimes she wondered if her mother and stepfather realized she was nearly seventeen. Probably not, since they treated her like she was Tommy's age.

She'd been trapped in the house all day with her little brother's friends who were spending the night for his birthday. Her mother had insisted she celebrate with the family. She'd already had her moment with Tommy that morning. She didn't need to stick around and play with first graders.

Alone time was most certainly a necessity at the moment. Besides, Mary had always loved to walk. She lived in a very small town in Iowa. Nothing much ever happened, so she didn't see why her parents, especially her mother's husband, had to be so dang strict all the time.

When that man laid down the law, her mother tended to fall in line. She'd been walking this road for years. He could get over trying to instill more rules. She had a little over a year to go and then she was out of there. If it weren't for Tommy, she would be so relieved to get away that she probably wouldn't even come back home at Christmas.

Already feeling calmer the farther she got from the house, Mary smiled as she noticed a couple birds chirping on the ice covered power line.

As she moved through the packed snow, she dropped petals from the red rose on the ground, leaving a trail behind her. When she turned and saw the beauty of red against the crisp white powder, it made her smile. Home could be boring at times, but it also could be peaceful and filled with so much beauty there weren't adequate words to explain it.

She continued walking as the sun lowered in the sky. She'd have to turn soon, but not yet. She wanted to reach the old power plant first. That would be a solid three-mile round-trip walk. She tugged her jacket a little bit tighter against her chest and kept on plugging forward.

When she heard tires on the crunchy snow behind her, Mary jumped, quickly spinning her head around and nearly slipping on the icy ground. There wasn't a lot of traffic on this backcountry road, but there was plenty of room for any vehicle to get around her. She spotted a large black SUV pulling up behind her and felt her first stirrings of unease. She quickened her pace.

"Hey!" someone yelled. She ignored him.

"Stop please. I need directions," the person continued. She slowed her pace and then turned around.

The person speaking looked to be only a few years older than she was. Not threatening at all. She weighed her options. She didn't trust strangers. But she also lived in a small town where you helped your neighbors.

"Where are you trying to get to?" she asked, not moving back toward the guy.

"It's up on Territorial I think. The address is smudged, but I have this map here," he said with a sheepish laugh.

Mary smiled. Yep, it was most likely some city slicker who didn't have a clue how to navigate country roads. Of course it was. No one in her small town as young as him would be driving an Escalade. That was a rich man's car. The teenagers lucky enough to get a car in her town drove old beat-up Ford pickups, and they liked them.

Rust added character, and if the vehicle had four different rims, that gave the person bonus points. Mary wondered how she was going to fare at a college in a city. She was a country girl, and she was a little bit afraid she wouldn't fit in with a crowd of people who drove vehicles like the one this guy was leaning on.

"Okay, let me look at the map," she said, finally moving toward him. He was out of the SUV, after all, and he had the map laid out on the hood.

"I really appreciate this. Are you from here?" he asked, his teeth chattering just a bit, making him appear even more charming.

As she got closer, she saw he couldn't be more than twenty at most. Not terrifying in the least. He was actually kind of cute. She brushed back her hair and wished she weren't wearing sweats and a hoodie. The last of her worries fell away. She was a track star. It wouldn't be difficult to run away if she felt she were in danger. But cute guys weren't dangerous, she assured herself.

"Yes, born and raised," she said with a depreciating laugh. As much as she mocked the city slickers, she wouldn't mind living in a big metropolitan area herself.

It sure would be better than cow tipping as a Saturday night activity.

"Very cool. I've never been here before," he said with a laugh. "Obviously."

She laughed with him as she leaned over the top of the SUV and looked at the map.

"How old is this thing?" she asked, trying to focus past the faded lines. She leaned in closer to get a better view.

"Just old enough," he said.

She picked up on the shift in his tone a moment too late. Suddenly there was intense pain in her head as something struck her on the back of the head. She didn't even have time to scream before the world went dark.

CHAPTER THREE

ARY CAME TO with a start. Immediately she sat up and swung around, trying to get her bearings. What was going on? Where was she? What had happened?

It was dark, too dark for her eyes to adjust, but as she squinted, trying to focus, she noticed a tiny bit of light coming in through a small window. She tried calming herself — not easy to do when she was petrified.

Slowly, her confined space came into focus. She was on a musty cot in a room where she could reach across and touch the other wall. The stench of urine, sweat, and other odors she was afraid to put a name to, drifted easily up her nostrils, making her gag. To top off all of that, her head was throbbing, and she desperately needed to use the bathroom.

But Mary was afraid to make a sound. She closed her eyes and tried thinking back. She'd been talking to the guy on the side of the road, then there had been extreme pain in her head before everything went black.

He had to have hit her, or he'd had someone else there; she hadn't seen who had hit her. But why? She couldn't figure that part out. If they had wanted to kill her, what was she doing in this musty room? She lay there for several moments as every bad scenario flashed through her mind.

She didn't want to contemplate what the man — or men — had in store for her. She was almost seventeen. She wasn't a fool. And right now, she thought death would be a better option than what might be coming her way.

Tears began falling from her closed eyelids, leaving wet trails on her dirty cheeks. She wasn't sure how much time had passed with her unconscious, but she knew it was enough that her mother was surely panicked, wondering where she was. And Tommy would be so upset. She'd promised to play a game of tag with him later that night.

"Mama . . ." she quietly sobbed, wondering why she'd been so mean the entire day. At this moment she'd give anything to hang out with Tommy and his friends.

Suddenly the door was wrenched open and light flooded into the tiny room, a man standing there in the opening.

"Good. You're awake."

Mary whimpered as he quickly approached, reaching out with gnarled fingers, harshly pulling her to her feet before she had even the smallest chance of slinking away from him.

"Please, I don't want to be here," she cried, his fingers bruising her skin.

"Yeah, well, life sucks," he answered with a chuckle before jerking her forward.

She lost her footing and fell to her knees, but he just yanked her back up, nearly pulling her shoulder from its socket. Pain shot through her body as he dragged her down a narrow hallway and up a set of squeaky stairs.

When they came out at the top, bright light invaded her eyes and several men were sitting around a table, two of them smoking, all of them holding a beer as they leered at her. She looked around, but the one who'd grabbed her was nowhere to be seen.

She didn't expect someone who drove such a nice vehicle to hang out in a filthy place like this, but where had he gone? She was trying to keep it together as she looked around for a weapon or a way to escape.

If they thought she was going down without a fight, they'd picked the wrong girl. But the odds of five to one didn't stack up in her favor.

"Are you sure we have to give this one up? I wouldn't mind keeping her for myself," one of the men said, his front tooth missing, his face unshaven.

"The boss already knows about her. So if you value your life, you'll keep your hands off," the man holding her snapped.

"I just want a little taste," the first man said as he stood and circled her, lifting his yellowed fingers and rubbing her cheek. She jerked away and gagged, which made the men laugh.

His tobacco and whiskey flavored breath rushed up her nostrils as he grabbed the back of her neck and pressed his disgusting lips against hers, his hand slapping her backside in a harsh crack.

She cried out, but that just made it possible for him to cram his tongue inside her cheek. She gagged again as bile rose in her throat, and he finally pulled back.

"Oh, yeah, I really want to keep this one," he said as he undid the top button of his pants and slid his fingers inside, looking like he was stroking himself in front of all of them. No one even blinked at his horrific behavior.

"I said she's spoken for. You do anything other than what you just did and you know the boss will kill us," he said. But he looked down at her with a similar look as he lifted a hand. "It really is too bad, though. She's real pretty."

Shaking where she stood, Mary refused to shed more tears as she glared at the man.

"Where are we? I demand to know where you're planning on taking me."

"Keep your damn mouth shut," the man snarled before raising his other hand and backhanding her, making her vision blur for a moment as she tasted blood in her mouth. She'd rather taste blood than his vile spit.

"No! I want to know where I am," she shouted back, struggling with the man still holding tightly to her arms. He wasn't releasing her, but as soon as the man who'd kissed her leaned forward again, she spit in his face, not caring about the consequences.

Fury rushed into his dark eyes as he glared at her with such hatred, she would have taken a step backward if she had been able.

His hand flew out and sharp pain slammed through her as he punched her hard in the chest, taking her breath away as she slumped down. Though she tried to hold herself together, the slight whimper escaping showed the group she was hurt and that made the ones sitting around the table laugh boisterously.

"I've got to get her ready," the man holding her said as he began marching her forward once again.

"I'll take over," another man from the table offered with a hopeful expression.

"Not going to happen," the obvious leader said.

She stumbled in front of him as he exited the kitchen and entered a dirty bathroom. The commode was covered in grime, the toilet paper wet, and the counter full of dirt. The sink and tub looked as if both hadn't ever been scrubbed. She recoiled from the smell alone — which unbelievably was worse than the bedroom she'd been pulled out of.

"Are the accommodations not to your liking, Princess?" the man asked with a harsh laugh. "You have two minutes. I'd use them wisely, because they will be your last. We're traveling for a very long time tonight."

He walked away from the door but didn't shut it. She saw his shadow in the hallway and knew he was standing right there. She'd either wet her pants or attempt to use the facility. As quickly as possible, and pulling her pants down only minimally, she hovered over the toilet and quickly did her business before she refastened her clothes.

The man was standing in the doorway when she looked up, an evil leer on his lips.

"It sure is a bummer to let you get away," he said as his eyes traveled across her young body.

She fought the tears wanting to fall. She wasn't going to give this man or any of the others anything else to laugh at. She would find a means to get away even if it was the last thing she ever did.

It wasn't just herself she was thinking about, either. It might be easier to give up if that were the case. But no. She had a promise to keep for her brother and one way or the other she was determined to do just that.

CHAPTER FOUR

MARY WAS BLINDFOLDED and tied up before being forced from the house and down a set of stairs. She was trying to remember everything she could, trying to hear the sounds around her, listening for anything that might give her a clue as to where she was.

She heard the rustling of trees, and the crunching of leaves. But not being able to see made it impossible for her to take in any clues to where she was. It truly seemed hopeless, not that she was going to give up so easily.

Before she could get her bearings, she heard a creaky door open and then she was pushed forward. She was lifted, and then the man was laying her down. She began to fight against him, but his fist connected with her jaw, nearly making her lose consciousness again as pain shot through her, and more blood oozed into her mouth.

She heard something above her snap shut, causing more fear to rush through her. Reaching her tied hands up, she discovered a solid wall above her. She reached to each side and found the same. She kicked out and there was nothing but walls.

Beginning to panic, she twisted from side to side as she tried to free herself. She was closed in completely. They must have placed her in a box — or possibly her own grave.

Her breathing came in pants as she struggled to free herself, but it was no use. Desperately she wiggled around until she didn't have the energy to struggle any further. She couldn't hear a sound. Whatever they'd put her in seemed to be soundproof.

But then she felt the vibration of movement. She stopped struggling and tried to pay attention. There was a bump of some sort and then just vibrating movement. She realized she must be in a box inside of a vehicle.

Okay, this wasn't good, but it didn't appear as if she were being buried alive — at least not yet. And thinking back, the man had said she was for someone. If that were the case, then surely they weren't going to be dropping her into the ground.

Although she might actually welcome death right now, she didn't want to die slowly, painfully, as she lost all oxygen or her body starved. She'd rather it went quickly so she could just sink into oblivion.

Mary slipped in and out of sleep as the hours slowly passed. She had no idea how much time had gone by, but when the lid to her box opened and a dim light shone above her, she took her first deep breath since she'd been placed in the soundless contraption.

"Welcome to your new home," the man said, an evil grin accompanying his words.

"Where's home?" she tentatively asked.

"Haven't you learned your lesson about asking questions?" he answered, reaching in and grabbing her hair, yanking her up to her feet.

It felt as if thick strands were being pulled from her head, but this time she didn't give him the satisfaction of tears. He seemed disappointed. He pulled her from the box, and she had only a moment to look at the tiny contraption her body had been crammed into before she was being yanked to the ground.

"Move it."

She fell to her knees when she tried to take a step. She'd been constricted in the tiny box for hours, and she couldn't walk. She tried standing and once again couldn't get back up. She didn't know what they expected from her. They were the ones who had entrapped her.

He gripped her arm again and dragged her forward. Finally her feet shuffled the tiniest bit, tingling shooting up her legs. None of the other men were around. She was somewhat grateful for that. But then again, what might this man try if he were the only one with her? She didn't want to find out.

"You're late."

The voice speaking wasn't one she'd heard before. It was almost formal, not as cruel as the other voices, but just as cold.

"I'm sorry. We had to wait until we knew the roads were clear," her captor said. "They put out a search on this one real quick."

"The boss doesn't like excuses." Then the man stepped forward and gave her an assessing look. "She's been beaten."

"She got a little out of hand, and I was forced to correct her," the man said.

"You know better than to touch the merchandise. The boss won't like this." A shiver traveled down Mary's spine as the new man looked her in the eyes for the first time. He circled around her, and the other man's hand fell away.

Mary thought for a moment about running, but as if the man knew, his lip turned up the slightest bit.

"Running will only get you injured," he said, his tone almost gentle. She found herself wanting to plead with him, beg him to let her go. He seemed as if he would understand.

"Please . . ." Her voice cracked on the one word.

"I'm just doing my job, little one. I can't do anything about it," the man said, his tone still soothing.

He then handed her captor an envelope, which the man opened before giving the well-dressed man a grin.

"It's a pleasure, as always, doing business with you," he said before he turned and walked away.

"Am I going to have trouble with you?" the well-dressed man asked.

Mary shook her head as she looked around. They were in the woods. Another van — this one much nicer — was parked about fifty feet away. It appeared as if it were only her and this new man. She was wrenching on the ties binding her hands. If she could just get them loose, she had a fair chance of getting away. She was sure she could outrun this man who appeared to be in his forties.

"I want to go home," she said when the ties didn't loosen.

"You are home now," he told her.

It was just the two of them, or so she thought.

"What in the hell is taking so long, Leo?" another voice called out.

"We're just getting to know each other, Rico," Leo responded, not taking his eyes off her.

The other man, Rico, approached, his eyes deadly cold. Mary found herself taking a step closer to Leo, who seemed to be the lesser of the two evils.

"She's trouble. I can always tell the troublemakers," Rico said with a grin, as if he enjoyed conflict. "Leo, get her secured. We still have a long way to go."

Mary's shoulders sagged. There was no way she was escaping both of these men. It didn't mean she wouldn't try if she had the chance. It just meant she was going to be hauled into another vehicle for now.

Rico grabbed her arm roughly and began tugging her toward the van.

"Please . . . I have to go to the bathroom," she said as he opened the back door.

"There aren't facilities out here," Rico said, his tone giving nothing away as to what he was thinking.

"I really have to go," she pleaded.

"Let her go. But I wouldn't let her out of your sight. This one's a runner. I can feel it," Leo said with a smile.

"Got it, boss," Rico replied. She was surprised. She'd thought Rico was the boss by the way he was acting.

Rico pulled her twenty feet away to a tree, in view of both men.

"Can I please just have a little privacy?" she attempted.

"You have one minute to get this done," Rico said.

"But my hands are tied. I can't get my pants down."

"Then I guess you're out of luck. You now have fifty seconds." The man looked at the watch on his wrist.

She knew he wasn't bluffing. She wiggled out of her sweatpants, doing the best she could with them both watching, humiliating herself even more. She quickly relieved herself before she pulled her pants back up, feeling disgusted.

"Let's go," Rico said as he glanced at his watch again.

Rico gripped her arm again and moved her to the van. Inside the back was a bench. The driver's area was caged off. She couldn't see past the wall separating it from the back.

Rico left her at the back with Leo then climbed in on the driver's side. Leo pushed her inside and then sat her on the bench. He reached for her ties, and Mary thought this might be the moment she could run. But before the thought was halfway out of her brain, the back doors sealed them in, and as soon as her ties were off, Leo grabbed one hand, threw a handcuff on it, and clipped it to the bar.

"We have a bit of a ride, so I wouldn't pull on that arm," Leo said as he leaned back, looking as if this were no more than another day at the office.

"Thanks," she sarcastically replied.

She knew it could earn her another slap, but she was furious.

Instead of the man striking out in anger, he laughed. "I think the boss will really enjoy you," he said, grinning at her.

"What does your boss want from me?" she asked after several minutes of silence. She wanted to know, yet she didn't. Although she would much rather be informed than not.

"It's what he does," Leo said with a sigh as he ran a hand over his face.

"What does he do?" she asked.

"He likes young girls," Leo said.

"What kind of monster is he?" she gasped.

"He's a very wealthy man who pretty much gets anything he wants," Leo told her. "If you don't fight this, just do what he wants, it'll be a lot less painful for you."

"Fight what? I don't even know what I'm fighting," she screamed.

"You know what this is about. The sooner you accept it, the better off you'll be," he told her.

"Please don't do this. I made a promise to my brother. I need to get back to him," she said, finally caving in to the tears again.

"I'm just doing my job," Leo told her.

"No, you're not!" she screamed. "You're kidnapping and abusing."

"Most people don't enjoy their work. They just do it," he said again.

"You're just as big a monster as your boss," she told him.

"I can be." The look in his eyes frightened her. She'd thought for a moment she had an ally in him. But it appeared she didn't. She had no one.

She didn't say anything else. What good would it do her anyway? Terror was sealing her throat.

She would escape. Mary was sure of it. She wouldn't let these people destroy her. She had a promise to keep. When the drugs they gave her kicked in and she began fading into sleep, she was grateful. She would get away from this reality any way she could.

"Stolen Innocence" is now available as a free download!

***Continue the Becoming Elena series with
"Forever Lost," now available!***

ABOUT CHRIS

Chris Alan never dreamed of becoming a writer, but sometimes fate throws a person a curve ball that you just so happen to catch, whether you want to or not. That's what happened for this breakout author who reviewers are calling "A Dark Poet Master." Already successful with a career as an electrician and a pilot, Chris is always looking for a new adventure, and stepping into the world of fiction has been his greatest one yet. For his first book, Dance in the Dark, he teamed up with author Melody Anne to scare their friends and family alike.

In his spare time Chris can either be found at the airport flying over his small town in the Willamette Valley of Oregon in his RV6, or coaching his son's baseball team. When Chris isn't writing, he's spending time with his family and friends having a bonfire, camping by a lake, or building something new at home. He loves to hear from all of you and can be found on Facebook and Instagram.

ABOUT MELODY

 Melody Anne is a NYT best selling author of the popular series: Billionaire Bachelors, Surrender, Baby for the Billionaire, Unexpected Hero's, Billionaire Aviators, Becoming Elena and some solo titles. She also has a Young Adult Series and is currently working on her first Thriller title to be released in 2017.

As an aspiring author, she wrote for years, then officially published in 2011, finding her true calling, and a love of writing. Holding a Bachelor's Degree in business, she loves to write about strong, powerful, businessmen and the corporate world.

When not writing, she spends time with family, friends, and her many pets. A country girl at heart, she loves the small town and strong community she lives in and is involved in many community projects.

To date, she has over 7 million book sales and has earned multiple placement on varying best seller lists, including NYT's, USA Today, and WSJ, being an amazon top 100 bestselling author for 3 years in a row, as well as a Kobo and iBooks best-seller. But beyond that, she just loves getting to do what makes her happy - living in a fantasy world 95% of the time.

See her website and subscribe to her newsletter at: www.melodyanne.com. She makes it a point to respond to all fans. You can also join her on her official facebook page: www.facebook.com/melodyanneauthor, or at twitter: @authmelodyanne. Also, follow her blog at author-melodyanne.blogspot.com.

.

Printed in Great Britain
by Amazon

81516826R00099